S0-BNI-560

MICHAEL Z. LEWIN

ASK THE
RIGHT QUESTION

THE MYSTERIOUS PRESS

New York • Tokyo • Sweden • Milan

Published by Warner Books

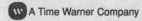 A Time Warner Company

Several people in Indianapolis responded graciously to my inquiries about the law, truth and custom of activities described fictitiously in this book. Discrepancies between the final product and reality are solely of my making and in no way reflect on the accuracy of what they told me or my appreciation of their efforts.

M.Z.L.

MYSTERIOUS PRESS EDITION

Copyright © 1971 by Michael Z. Lewin
All rights reserved.

Cover design by Andrew Newman
Cover illustration by Mike Fisher

This Mysterious Press Edition is published by arrangement with the author.

The Mysterious Press name and logo are trademarks of Warner Books, Inc.

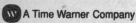 Mysterious Press books are published by
Warner Books, Inc.
666 Fifth Avenue
New York, New York 10103

A Time Warner Company

Printed in the United States of America

First Mysterious Press Printing: June, 1991

10 9 8 7 6 5 4 3 2 1

To Maz
Newton (née Piglet)
and
Alan Lebowitz

ASK THE
RIGHT QUESTION

1

I had a big decision after lunch. Whether to read in the office or to stay in my living room and read.

It was one of those decisions that tell you about yourself, how much self-indulgence you allow. The room I live in is nicer than the office. The chair is softer, it's a shorter walk for a glass of orange juice. On the other hand two o'clock is still business hours whether there is business or not. And should a client accidentally stumble through my door, it wouldn't do to be dozing by the window in the back.

I made a virtuous choice. I took the pillow off my bed and carried it through to the squat rectangular light-green room I call my office. I put the pillow on the seat of my swivel chair and then I put me on the pillow. "Now I lay me down to sleep . . ."

And I commenced, for the eighth consecutive day, an afternoon read. Fourteen days into it, the October of 1970 was looking like the slowest month in my detecting history.

By half past four I was awake again and debating whether to move back to the living room. It was a day filled with such problems. Office hours were till five, but the afternoon movies start at four thirty.

But then the unusual happened. A client walked in.

I must have looked surprised, because she hesitated, clinging to the door. She raised an eyebrow and said, "Should I have knocked?" It was clear from the tone of her voice that she knew perfectly well that the outside door bore the words "Walk Right In." When I first opened the office I was more buoyant than I have proved to be day in, day out. My water line has risen considerably.

"No, no," I said. "Come in. Sit down."

She paused over the dusty chair and then sat down gingerly. Indianapolis is one of the polluted cities; chairs get dusty very fast between clients.

She was young. Shoulder-length walnut hair. Violet-tinted glasses. A green jacket and pants, a suit-type thing.

I got my notebook out from the desk's top drawer and I opened it.

"It smells in here," she said.

I sighed. I prepared for rapid disenchantment. I flipped my notebook closed.

"Stop. Don't do that. Please! I want you to find my biological father."

In our few seconds' acquaintance I hadn't noticed the tension that had been gripping her, but now I felt positive relaxation passing through her body. A young body, budding with taste and moderation.

"Your what?" I asked mildly.

"My biological father!" A deep furrow split the tinted lenses. "You are the Albert Samson it says on the door, aren't you?"

Her presumption did not excite me: that The Real Albert Samson trades uniquely in finding biological fathers. I patronized her.

"I am indeed Albert Samson, my dear. But won't you find your biological father at home with your biological mother?" In bed? With the blinds drawn?

"No," she said definitively. "That is precisely where I won't find him. Will you take the job? Will you find my biological father for me?"

Physically she was squirming in her chair. Rubbing the dust in. And mentally she was race-horsing, moving ahead far faster than I wanted to. She looked, maybe, twenty. But her emotional control—lack of it—suggested a maiden of fewer summers.

Reopening my notebook, I said, "First things first. I'll need your name and address."

"I am Eloise Crystal. I live at 7019 North Jefferson Boulevard."

I duly soiled a fresh page with these facts and the date. That made it official.

"And how old are you?"

She bristled slightly. "Is that usually the second question you ask your clients?" Either she was touchy about how old she was or she was a representative of the Women's Age Liberation Movement. "I have money," she continued. "I can pay you if that's what you mean."

"I'll need to know your age," I said.

"I'm sixteen."

I'll swear she looked older, but I guess such perceptions have passed me by.

"What time is it?" she asked.

I gestured to my cuckoo, behind her and next to the office door. It's genuine Swiss, a leaf from my salad days. We read it together. 4:42.

"I have to go soon. Will you do it? Will you take the job?"

"Look, Miss Eloise Crystal of Jefferson Boulevard, how do you think these things work? Do you think you just walk in here and say, 'Find my biological daddy,' and then come back in a week to pick him up? From what you've told me just how the hell am I supposed to know whether I can find your so-called biological father or not?"

"You don't have to swear," she said prissily. She was upset. That was just as well. I'm not too keen on pushy people, and for pushy little girls I have a very low tolerance.

"Just what is it that you want me to try to do, and second, can you give me one good reason why I should do it?"

I was beginning to get through. She started crying.

She sobbed uncontrollably for three minutes, snuffled for two and caught her breath for about one and a half. I didn't have much else to do besides watch her and the clock. And write in the notebook, "Client cried; may be crazy bananas." And then feel a little bad about the whole thing. Part of it had to be my mistake. If I realized she was a kid from the start maybe I would have been more flexible. Kids don't know much about dealing with people. For that matter, people don't know that much about dealing with kids. So why don't you hear her out, Albert? I told myself. She thinks you can help her with something. Maybe you can.

I almost went into the living room to get her a piece of paper towel to dry her eyes. But I didn't, because I was afraid, a gut reaction, that if I left the office she might not be there when I got back.

As it turned out she had a handkerchief of her own. She pulled it out of a little purse I hadn't noticed before.

When she was about dried out I said, "I'd like you to tell me about it." It was my best offer.

She just took a breath in and blinked her eyes. Carefully she put the glasses on again. I guess she liked them on. Apparently you can't cry without taking glasses off. They were prescription.

Trying to be gentle and fatherly (I am a father after all) I took a shot and said, "Did your parents wait until now to tell you something important?"

Add drivel and get instant fury. "*They* never told me anything! *They* say he is my father, I mean, they never said anything else. But I know he isn't. I *know* it! I have proof."

11

"Proof" is a word that grabs my attention. Proving things is nice, I like it. The problem is that so many things that people "prove" don't stay proved.

"What sort of proof?"

"I have blood proof," she said. "His type is B; my mother's is O; and I have A. That means he *can't* be my father. It's not scientifically possible!" Her tone was plaintive. I was recording the information.

"Who can't be your father?"

"He can't. I mean, Leander Crystal can't."

"He is the man who lives with your mother?"

"That's right."

"What's your mother's name?"

"Fleur. Fleur Graham Crystal."

"She's married to Leander?"

"Yes."

"They live with you? At"—I consulted my notes—"at 7019 Jefferson Boulevard?"

"That's right."

"How long have they been married?"

"For, I don't know exactly, twenty or twenty-one years."

"So they were married when you were born?"

"That's right."

"But you think Leander Crystal is not your father?"

"I *know* Leander Crystal is not my father. The blood types prove it."

I looked at them again. I did flunk genetics in college once, but I know enough about elementary blood typing to have investigated my way through two paternity cases in the last seven years. For a kid to have A-type blood, there has to be some A in the parents. She had said the parents were B and O.

"Where did you get the blood types from?"

She smiled. The first smile in our acquaintance. A nice knowing smile. "I did them myself. In school. And I had Mr. Shubert—he's my bio teacher—he checked it."

She flushed slightly. What with the smiles and the flushing I figured the phony hard core had bit the dust. She was more relaxed, more girlie. I liked her.

"Well, actually *I* only typed my blood and my, well, Leander's. I got

12

Mummy's when the doctor was at the house two weeks ago. She, Mummy, had a miscarriage. The doctor said he was afraid she would need a transfusion." Shyly my client added, "They . . . it was twins."

"Your parents must have been upset."

She nodded vigorously. "Mummy especially. I would have liked twins."

My cuckoo cheeped five times and Eloise started.

"Does that thing tell the right time?"

"More literally than most clocks," I said. And then I said yes to answer the question I had been asked. In my business you get pretty fussy about things like that.

"I have to go." She stood up, and I rose to face her. My pillow fell off the chair behind me but I had no regrets. "I came here from school and they'll be worried if I'm not home soon. Are you going to do it for me? Will you find my biological father?"

"I can't possibly tell you. The most I could say now is that I will try, and I can't even say that until I know a lot more than you've told me."

She opened her purse and pulled out a piece of money which she thrust at me.

"Here's a hundred dollars. How much trying will that get?"

Businessmen have said things like that to me before, but I was astonished to hear it from Eloise Crystal. Maybe she was telling me something about the environmental father she'd grown up with.

"You just hang on to that for the moment. If you're interested, I charge thirty-five dollars per eight-hour day, plus expenses."

"Please take it. Please!" The hand holding the bill was wavering. "It's mine. I didn't steal it or anything. I have money. That's not a problem."

I took the bill and put it on my desk.

"I'll keep it for you. But before I can even think about taking your case I've just got to have more information from you. What time do you get out of school tomorrow?"

"Oh, I don't have to go to school," she said.

I sighed. Some client problems are peculiar to minors. I said, "I have other things to do too. What time do you get out of school?"

"I can be here about four. I—I didn't come straight up today. I wasn't . . . sure. You know?"

"I know."

We had reached a plateau. Our mutual understanding flowed like wine. I decided to sip a little.

"How did you get a blood sample from Leander?"

"It wasn't easy," she said. "But if you want something bad enough, there's usually a way. See you tomorrow."

She swept out of the office.

Whatever else she was, she was quick on her feet.

My quarters serve me admirably, but they are not in the right part of the building to let me watch a client leaving downstairs. My only window is in my living room and it fronts on Alabama Street. It gives me an eastern panorama over the White Star Diner and a Borden's Ice Cream factory.

The front of my building is on Ohio Street. The office next to mine has two fine windows overlooking Ohio, and they are very convenient. The office is vacant and has been for the last three years. My landlord can't find a sucker to pay twenty dollars a month more for a two-window northern exposure than I pay for my one shot to the east. He's suggested on occasion that I become that sucker, but I fend him off. Not that I couldn't afford the twenty dollars, usually. But I am versed enough in lock manipulations to be able to get in there whenever I want to. For a bath, say, or to look at a client from above. Besides, I wouldn't want to look out my window every day and see the Wulsin Building right across the street. And my ivies grow better in an eastern window than they would to the north.

I didn't know how fast Eloise Crystal would get down, so I hurried. I needn't have. I'd been plopped on the windowsill for more than a minute when a prim little Miss Eloise appeared on the sidewalk below me and turned left. I opened the window and leaned gingerly out. She walked the three blocks to Meridian and there turned left again. Either she had conned me about having to go home or she had no car and was heading for a bus. If it was the bus I hoped she had something smaller than a hundred to give the driver.

I closed the window and got up off the sill. I retraced the footfalls to my office. I closed my outer door, bolted it, and ambled to the inner room of my private life.

14

But before I got settled I remembered my notebook. I went back to the office to get it. I also picked up the hundred-dollar bill and, for lack of a better place, I put it in my wallet. Then I went back to my living room.

You can see how much I must have saved in bus fares since I decided to move into the back room here.

2

Eloise Crystal had left my office a little after five. By eight I had finished dinner and my daily housecleaning. It was evening project time and tonight had been assigned to work on crossword puzzles. Writing puzzles is one of the ways I supplement my income a little. Not that it is really lucrative, but if you have to pass the time anyway you might as well pick up a buck or two.

I do a number of things besides detecting which bring in a little money from time to time. I'm a bit of a photographer, a bit of a carpenter, a bit of a gambler, and I sometimes do odd jobs for odd friends. But I am primarily a private investigator—that's what my passport says. I've been at it for seven years and I'm proud.

Seven whole years, a record.

And in the whole time I'd never had a little girl come in and ask me for her biological pa.

I chewed on my crossword pencil and thought about her for a while. What were the odds she wouldn't show up again?

Hard to tell. Maybe evens.

And if she remembered to appear?

Hmmmm. Tell her to take her problem elsewhere? I thought about the "problem." Just how the hell would I set about finding a long-lost biological father anyway?

She's sixteen. So we would be looking for a human male known to have committed a brief act sixteen years ago with the mother of Eloise Crystal. That would be Fleur Crystal. That would be about seventeen years ago; nine months for gestation.

And this human male is not the one most readily available, Leander Crystal.

15

So what else is there?

Nothing. We know nothing about the man. Not even that he is still alive. Not even that Fleur ever really knew him other than in the Biblical sense.

No more facts at all.

So add probability. *Probably* Fleur was extensively acquainted with the father of her child. *Probably* somebody somewhere knew of Fleur and the man and of the essence of their relationship, if not necessarily of the conception.

Probability gave way to possibility. *Possibly* it all took place in Indianapolis. *Possibly* the man is still around, maybe someone client Eloise already knows. Like a friend of the family's. Like a good friend . . .

My speculations flickered and were blown out by the same breath that uttered the word "conceivably."

Replaced by more practical thoughts. What would one do to get a lead?

Check friends of the mother to get an idea of what sort of woman she is, and was. What sort of things she did, where she went, the important periods in her life. And what she was doing about seventeen years ago.

Replaced by more practical thoughts yet. The whole business would rest on the validity of Eloise's blood test reports.

But how do you check a family's blood types? Send a nurse to the house to collect blood before breakfast?

I went back to my crossword puzzle.

Half an hour later, having reminded myself of the hundred dollars resting in the generous confines of my wallet, I decided to give Eloise the tentative benefit of the doubt. The benefit of a little simple background work, since I didn't exactly have a whole lot else to do. Maybe by tomorrow if I was really sure I knew exactly what it was that she wanted me to do and why she wanted it done, maybe tomorrow if I could reassure myself about those blood tests, maybe tomorrow I would take the case, formally.

Tonight, tentative, I hit the phone to Maude Simmons, the Sunday editor of the Indianapolis *Star*. I dialed her private line there, the one she uses for her private business.

"Simmons."

I identified myself.

"Berrtie! How the hell are you?" Rolling the *r*: I hate that. She knows it.

"I'm down at police headquarters. They're holding me for assaulting an editrix. I need somebody to keep the other prisoners from picking on me."

"Oh," she said. "That's nice. Pity I haven't time. Can I help you with something else?"

"Yeah. A little information."

"Surprise, surprise."

"On some people named Crystal."

"The rich Crystals? Leander and Fleur Graham?" She was ahead of me already.

"I guess so, if they have a daughter named Eloise and live on Jefferson Boulevard."

"That's them. How deep and when?"

"How about whatever you know off the top of your head and now?"

"Poor Berrtie. Don't you ever get real jobs?" She paused. I thought she was waiting for me to answer that. I ignored the silence. I make my own bed and I lie in it.

But instead she said, "You wouldn't believe it."

"What?"

"The pneumatic tube contraption here just presented me with today's livestock report. Did you know that calves closed unchanged in Chicago? Eight hundred thousand dollars for a tube system and it brings me the livestock report. It's enough to make you cry."

We gave it a few moments silence. Maude hates wastes of money.

"You got your notebook?"

"I have it."

"Well, first off they're rich. I mean real millions, plural, rich. I can find out how rich if you want."

"No, thanks, little fella, not just now. What are they like?"

"Well, pretty quiet."

"Meaning?"

"Meaning no current gossip pertaining to behavior the *Star* would consider immoral. And no past gossip that I remember. Is it a divorce gig? If so you're in pretty big money."

I was ashamed to tell her that I was on the verge of being hired by the kid. "No divorce. Not sure what this is going to be yet."

"Poor Berrrtie."

"Tell me something interesting. Anything."

"Well, I remember stories about Fleur's old man. That was Estes Graham, and that's where the money came from by the way. He died '53 or '54, but for years he gave big birthday bashes, and everyone in town would turn out for them. The only problem was that there wasn't a drop of anything alcoholic at them. There's a guy still on the paper who went to one, I think it was in '50. He took his own hip flask. Old Estes Graham spotted it and he got his son-in-law, that would be Leander Crystal, he got Crystal to toss this guy out personally. But that's about the only thing I have offhand. I can tell you that the Crystals, both of them, live very quiet lives. None of the usual society, charity stuff most folks with their kind of cash get roped into."

"That's it?"

"That's all I have off the top of my head. I can put my staff on it and give you a lot more detail. We have quite a research organization, if you can give us a little help on whatever it is you really want."

"I'm afraid that for the moment I'll have to leave it at that. How much?"

"Oh, just a token. Whatever you think is fair. Generous, but fair."

We hung up.

I went to my living-room desk and got an envelope. I thought about putting a dime in it, but for the future's sake I decided not to fun around. I wrote out a check for five dollars and sent it to Miss Simmons, care of the Indianapolis *Star*.

Maude is quite a gal. Ancient, profane, hard-drinking and avaricious. She's also a boon to the thirty or so private-detective offices in Indianapolis. From her nerve center as Sunday features editor at the *Star* her real business is supplying news to private parties. The stuff that's not fit to print: personal backgrounds, credit information, household secrets. She has a network of people with ears and talents. And she makes money with it. Not usually from two-bitters like me, though I've done some real business with her too. She says the police have used her services; I am not accustomed to disbelieve.

I left my notebook at the phone table, but my mind was just not on the crossword puzzle wavelength. I wished it were Thursday, instead of Wednesday. Not so much because I would know better where I stood with Eloise *et al.*, but because the Pacers would be playing. First game of the season as defending champs of the American Basketball Association. I am a basketball fan and the Pacers' radio broadcasts come in very handy for passing the long winter nights. Sometimes, when I am lucky and the sports photographers are indisposed, I get a call to take some basketball pics. I develop black and white in my office closet, and apart from spot free-lancing, the camera stuff helps in the PI work too. Bits of a life can dovetail.

I tried to put aside my thoughts of Crystals. But there weren't too many concrete thoughts to put aside. From what Maude had given me it seemed that Fleur was a quiet one. And therefore, perhaps, dangerous?

And Eloise? A girl-woman. Adolescence makes for a biologically based dual personality. Perhaps the real question was: Which half was the one that wanted to hire me? And how much chance there was that the blood typings turned out to be exactly as advertised. But mine was not to weep and wonder. I could wait until the morrow.

I set aside my crossword puzzle for the last time and wrote a letter to my daughter. I told her about some rabbits and bears I talked to recently. Very nice, unsymbolic rabbits and bears who got along well and slapped their knees after they told jokes. My daughter is nine now. Maybe a little old to talk to rabbits and bears. Fathers can't be expected to know everything.

Taking the book I'd used in the afternoon, I went to bed.

3

I woke up about eight and made myself a cheese omelet. It was a poor imitation of the ones my ex-wife used to make but one makes sacrifices to preserve integrity.

I thought about how to pass the day. Not real thought; I'd already decided to put in a little time on Miss Crystal against the chance I took her offer of employment. It's not that I had anything more notable to do.

I did decide to do it easy and with a little class. No stress and no strain. I gathered my notebook and writing instrument and went out for a leisurely stroll. West down Ohio Street to Pennsylvania Avenue. Then North up Pennsylvania. The route took me through Indianapolis's ideological heartland. Within oblique sight of the Soldiers and Sailors Monument in the Circle. On a clear day you can see for blocks from the top. Past the post office and Federal Building, the *Star-News* Building, and the YWCA. Past the World War Memorial, a graveled city block with an obelisk in the middle and cannons on the corners. Past the National Headquarters of the American Legion.

And finally to St. Clair Street. Where I entered, at long last, the Indianapolis-Marion County Public Library.

I spent a lot of time there as a kid. It was cool even in the summers and it was quiet. And of all those books, each one representing hundreds of hours of work, some had even worked for me.

But I hadn't come at nine o'clock to be first in line for the latest worst seller. I headed immediately for the microfilm files of the Arts Division on the second floor.

There are six microfilm viewers on the south wall of the Arts Division. But at that time in the morning there wasn't much demand for them, so I got one of the two at the right, next to the microfilm cabinets. Without having to walk very far I could examine all the microfilm I cared to.

I looked over the scant notes I had from Eloise and Maude. I decided first to find the marriage of Fleur and Leander Crystal.

It was twenty or so years ago. I started with the *Star* for January of 1949, fitted it into the viewer and started cranking. I checked each day's social page in a leisurely elegant manner, stopping elsewhere only to sample the heady world of 1949 sports.

In the February 13 issue I found an unexpected bonus. A story of the annual birthday party for Estes Graham. One of the man's wild teetotal wingdings. ". . . well catered and handled with the restraint and decorum we have come to expect from Estes Graham. . . ." It read like a small-town theater review: the ushers and the props mistress did real good.

On February 12, 1949, Estes Graham had become seventy-eight years old.

I cranked on. A regular little butterfly I was, flitting from social page to social page.

At 10:35 (June 3, 1949) I found the announcement of the wedding: "Fleur Olian Graham to Wed."

Not a large story. No picture. But it was specific. The wedding would take place September 6. The lucky man was Leander Crystal of Ames, Iowa. The reception would be held in Estes Graham's home on North Meridian Street.

What more sensible than to jump immediately and see if the wedding had gone off as scheduled?

September 7, 1949. "Graham Heiress Weds."

There was a picture this time. That was good. In my heart I like pictures best.

They were coming out of church. Fleur and Leander Crystal, standing with Estes Graham.

Fleur was at her new husband's right. She grinned furiously. An attractive girl, hair that photographed dark. Face a little round. But with careful, articulated lips, in black and white, her best feature. I studied the picture. I thought I would probably be able to recognize her.

Leander was about Fleur's height. He stood stiffly beside her in his Army uniform. I was surprised he was only a sergeant, but the uniform bore medals and it fit him well. His most striking physical characteristic was his virtually complete baldness.

Estes was in his turn at Fleur's right. Leaning on a cane, head slightly stooped. The three heads drew a level line. He was old, and had been for all of Fleur's life, if the picture did not lie. He wore a tux with very long tails.

The story with the photo included an extensive description of the wedding and reception, as well as biographies and plans.

The biographies provided the following.

Fleur was nineteen. She was graduated in 1946 from Tudor Hall, which was a private girls' school in Indianapolis. She had done some volunteer hospital work as a high school student late in the war and she had continued the volunteer work afterward. She had attended the

21

Butler University College of Nursing for a year, but was interrupting her studies to marry.

Crystal, at twenty-nine, had just graduated *cum laude* from Butler University's Business College. He had served in Europe and had been awarded a Silver Cross and a Purple Heart. Presumably he came to Indianapolis to study on the GI Bill. Nothing was stated about his career plans. Perhaps with Estes Graham and a business degree, that was understood.

The couple would spend the night in Estes' house and then leave for a month-long honeymoon in Florida.

By the time I finished making my notes, it was nearly eleven o'clock and time for decision. Break for an early lunch, or go on and try to find another chunk of information?

A rare burst of ambition took hold of me. I decided to stay.

From the wedding I cranked on. The first mention of familiar names was on October 18. It was in the caption of a picture of Leander and Fleur getting off a plane. The bride and bridegroom at Weir Cook Airport returning from the Florida honeymoon. Both smiling this time, no doubt from memories of the Miami sun and the Miami moon. I liked this picture. It made me feel better about the bond between Leander and his apparently errant wife. Newly wed can be a happy time.

As I cranked my way to the end of the year it occurred to me that there was a slightly more efficient way to go about things. There were three more events of significance to the family that I knew existed: Eloise's conception, Eloise's birth, and the death of Estes Graham.

If Eloise was sixteen now, then her birth took place in 1954 or the end of '53. The conception nine months earlier. And Graham had died, according to Maude, in '53 or '54.

The whole thing came to me in a flash! At the annual birthday party of 1953, some crude reporter had gotten Fleur drunk on illicit hooch, and then had knocked her up. Leander had been occupied elsewhere at the time, and Fleur was too ashamed to tell him or her father that she had been drinking. Later when she found she was pregnant, nobody knew that the father wasn't Leander, until Eloise had stumbled on it. End of case. Reporters can be such bounders!

I took a look at the social pages of February 13, 1954, in search of a birthday party.

There was nothing. Presumably no party. Estes either dead or sick. Or for reasons I did not know, uninclined to celebrate his eighty-third.

I cranked backward in time, day by day. This time checking both sociable pages and obits.

I got as far back as October 2, 1953, before I found anything. And that was a picture of Fleur, Leander and Estes, back at Weir Cook Airport. The Crystals leaving for France. No indication of how long they would be away. Just that they were going to visit some of the ground Leander had covered in the war. And to visit the place where Fleur's older brother Joshua had died in the same war.

The picture also showed that Estes had been alive in October, '53, and presumably for his birthday too.

I knew why Estes hadn't held his annual soirée: he couldn't get a decent bouncer to replace Leander.

So the old man had to have died after his eighty-third birthday. I cranked back to February '54 and started the social-obit circuit going the other way.

The job was getting morbid. I found the obituary of a kid I'd gone to grade school with. I hoped that Fleur and Leander got back before Estes went.

And at 11:50 I was rewarded for my charity. April 18, 1954. Fleur and Leander returned to Weir Cook after their long sentimental journey. I counted fingers. They had been gone for six and a half months.

I decided I'd had enough for a while. I broke for lunch.

After refilling the cartons of microfilm I headed for fresh air and sunlight. Better make that just plain air and sunlight. On the way out I stopped in a phone booth and called my own number. My answering service reported, sleepily, that there had been no calls of any kind for me all morning. That was mildly depressing. It would make nine days without ordinary business.

For lunch I had to choose between quality and convenience. Having resolved to live the day with a degree of class, I opted for quality. That meant Joe's Fine Food, and a walk of five blocks to the corner of Vermont and Illinois.

Joe's has only been around for a few years, but it's one of the best joints in the city for lunch. Especially on Monday and Tuesday, when it specializes in Mexican food. But even on Thursday, it is good enough for a man of quality.

I was moderately lucky to get a counter seat near the door. The place was packed. It really takes something for a lunch joint to be packed. I know about things like that because my mother runs a luncheonette.

I ordered a cheeseburger with other delicacies. And took a drag on a glass of water.

I reflected on the Crystals' European tour. They'd been gone for nearly seven months. If Eloise was sixteen, the odds were good that she had been conceived in Europe.

That realization did a creditable job of depressing me.

Looking for a biological father is hard enough when you have a finite number of boyfriends sniffing around a young girl's door. But when the girl was impregnated nearly seventeen years ago while traveling in Europe, the choice of biological fathers is dazzling.

I ate my meal with resignation and with a good deal less relish than I had expected.

If my conjecture was right, if Eloise was born between about the middle of June, 1954, and, say, the middle of December, she was conceived on a foreign shore. And in that case it was probably best to cut losses—half a day's work—and let her find a big detective agency with contacts abroad. But me?

I had an extra coffee.

Ah, well. Something that looks like an interesting case walks in the door, during a period which is otherwise a drought, and then it walks out again.

I had another coffee. And mentally I let my head sink to the counter.

Ah, well. Don't let's hurt other folks. I left a big tip, and went back into the autumn sun.

All problems at the beginning are too big to grasp. The important knack is to break them down into individual soluble parts. To ask the right questions.

Just what questions had I asked? Only "Where was the mother at the time of conception?" So I hadn't gotten an answer I wanted. So big deal.

I hadn't even asked the real question. I hadn't gone to Fleur Crystal and asked her straight. Maybe she would tell me. Maybe if I charmed

24

her. Or tricked her. There were all kinds of possibilities. All kinds of things I could do.

I increased my stride. One of the questions I had to ask was whether the blood typings were the way Eloise said they were.

I picked up the microfilm reels for April, 1954, through December, 1954. And I cranked inexorably on, more aggressive than I had been in the morning.

On June 3 I learned that Fleur Crystal was expecting. Eloise's first appearance. The baby and heir was due in the middle of October. I counted fingers to reveal that the conception was located roughly mid-February, 1954. Right in the middle of a cold French winter.

I did not jump straight to October. I was still interested in finding Estes' death. And I was also interested in the possibility of one of those wretched rituals called a baby shower. I might pick out a useful friend or two to talk about Fleur with.

But I never got to wet my mind with a baby shower. All through the summer none was reported. I found Estes Graham's obituary instead. He died of a heart attack on August 20, 1954. He had not lived to see his granddaughter.

The obit gave me my first information about Fleur's mother. She was the former Irene Olian, daughter of a Reverend Billy Lee Olian. She had married Estes in 1916 and had given him four children. Three sons, Windom, Sellman, and Joshua. And the daughter, Fleur. All three sons had been killed in World War II. But Irene Olian Graham had already died in 1937. Estes was survived only by Fleur and Leander and Eloise *in utero*.

I thought about the wedding picture. Especially about Leander Crystal getting married in his uniform. Crystal was the perfect son-in-law for a man who'd lost three sons in war. About the right age, something of a hero himself, and alive.

Estes' funeral was scheduled for August 23.

I cranked on.

To a surprise. In the innards of Friday, August 27, I found another picture of Fleur and Leander at Weir Cook Airport. Leaving, according to the caption, for New York City. Not happy. Fleur, clearly pregnant, dressed in black. No additional story.

25

Not a very good time to go to New York. They certainly didn't travel places in the comfortable seasons. A French winter and a New York summer.

The only thing I could think of was that there was some complication in Fleur's pregnancy. So they were going to New York to birth the child.

There was no notice of Eloise's birth in the *Star* between August 27 and October 31, 1954. That gave me a moment's hesitation. But I decided to check out the New York records. I got the New York *Times* microfilms out and began a search there.

I finally found her. Born, November 1, 1954, a daughter, Eloise Graham Crystal, to Leander and Fleur Crystal of Indianapolis, Indiana.

I had to laugh. Yesterday had been October 14, 1970. That gave me a fifteen-year-old client, not a sixteen-year-old one. She had hedged by a few days. Poor thing.

Of course in some states those few days make all the difference.

I went back to the *Star*. And found, on November 16, a picture of the family Crystal returning to Indianapolis. Eloise's first introduction to Indianapolis. The airport photographer was on the ball. His combings of the names of people with reservations and the names on the incoming flight lists had yielded some pictures that I appreciated.

From November 16 on I found only one item more.

December 30, 1954. Notice of the completion of probate of Estes' will. Worth in the neighborhood of twelve million. Nice neighborhood.

With that I packed up shop. It was pushing three. I was expecting Eloise Crystal, and had a call to make before I saw her. I refiled all the microfilm, gathered my notes and walked briskly home.

4

First thing back in the office, I called Clinton Grillo. He's one of my lawyers, the one I use for actual and possible criminal prosecution of my nearest and dearest. Me. His secretary asked me to hold on. Which I did, for nearly ten minutes.

The question I needed answering was whether I was legally free to take on a fifteen-year-old female client.

"You've come up with some interesting questions in your time Albert. Is this one hypothetical?" He is also the father of one of my closer high school friends.

"No, sir, it's not."

"I am presuming the young lady wishes to employ you without the knowledge of her parents."

"That is correct."

"Well, I know of no specific prohibitions, but there would seem to be many dangers. For instance, you would have no legal recourse should such a client decide to withhold payment of monies owed you. And were she to visit you alone in your office you would be particularly vulnerable should such a client take it into her head to make sexual accusations. Especially, shall we say, if someone else had already done what the client decided to accuse you of."

"You have a dirty mind, sir."

"True, my boy. How true."

"That's it?"

"Isn't it enough for you to think about?"

"Guess so."

It all depends on just how much you trust the minor client. How serious you believe it is and how likely to turn sour.

Eloise Crystal arrived at my office ten minutes before four o'clock. By doing so she gave me a time measure of the hesitation which preceded her arrival at 4:25 the day before.

But the difference was more than one of time. Confidence declared itself in her walk, in the efficiency with which she took the chair. Today the chair was her own. The net impression was the inverse of her last visit. Today she dressed younger—skirt, blouse, sandals, no shades— but she radiated more maturity. An assured young woman. My fifteen-year-old chamelion.

"Well," she said. "How are we doing? Found his name yet?"

She was joking, but I also suspected that she knew little of the tedium and irresolution of the world. Today's joke might be a serious inquiry next week and I could easily have just as little to tell her.

"I did do a little work today, as a matter of fact. But we still haven't settled whether I'm really going to work for you or not."

She dropped her head a little, and said, "I know. But I've been thinking about it, and I'm really glad that I decided to come yesterday. It's a load off my mind somehow. That I've finally taken a positive step to get it all solved."

"I thought you only found out about those blood types in the last couple of weeks."

She nodded. "But I've always known something was wrong. Before, I just didn't know what."

"Wrong with you?"

"Yeah. Something about me that made it bad between them. Like, I used to think I was an orphan."

Almost everybody does. "And what do you think now?"

She paused and tried to get it right, the way she felt it. "I think, well, that Leander knows that I'm not his and that he's sort of repressed my mother for it."

Repressed? "Don't they get along?"

"They don't really not get along. But they don't do anything together. They don't smile at each other. He goes off to work in the morning and sometimes doesn't come back till late. Mummy worries a lot that she's sick. And they don't have any friends."

She resented it. Parents should have friends.

My cuckoo sounded off four times.

I leaned back in my chair and put my foot up on the bottom desk drawer edge. It's one of my favorite thinking positions. "Eloise," I said. It was the first time I had said her name.

"I'm listening," she said. She wasn't happy.

"You see, I'm in a difficult position. Basically that is because the particular problem you want me to solve is one which I can't be sure I can solve. I could work for weeks and not have any information that would help you. And that runs into money, pretty big money."

"I understand that. I have money. I have a trust fund that my grandfather made for me."

"The problem is that you might be spending a lot for nothing."

"I don't care. I don't have anything else I want that I can spend it on."

28

Which seemed fair enough, as a matter of fact.

"Another thing is that you might be better off with one of the big agencies. I'm just one man."

"I tried one of them," she said. "One with a big ad in the yellow pages."

"What did they tell you?"

"They wouldn't take me seriously. They weren't rude or anything, but they just said they couldn't help me and that I should go to my parents and ask them."

"That might not be bad advice."

"Oh, I just couldn't do that." She shuddered. "The man at the agency just thought I was crazy." She gave me a smile. "At least that's some progress I'm making. You don't think I'm crazy, do you?"

"No, I don't," I said honestly. "But I will have to check the blood typings you gave me."

"But why?" she said heatedly. "They're right. I did them myself." Defending her handiwork. An attitude I like.

"That's the point. I would have to check them myself. As you've outlined things the entire investigation would depend on the accuracy of those blood types. With any crucial facts it is essential to check them and cross-check them."

"OK," she said. "Will you do it?"

A question I hadn't really answered in my mind. There was one more set of conditions that needed to be met, but I could hardly ask her for some way to prove her personal reliability. For one reason because she was not really competent to evaluate it.

"Let's do it this way," I said. "I will take your job, but with the following limitations. It will be on a day-to-day basis. I'll keep working as long as I think I am finding out things that might be useful. But no longer."

"So you'll take it?"

"On those conditions."

"Oh, I'm so glad. I was afraid there for a minute that you were going to send me away too."

"I may."

"But not for a while. I'm so glad. I just feel sure that you're going to settle it all for me."

"I guess it's time to undermine your confidence," I said. "Here's my first report. I've found out that you were conceived in Europe, probably France, during the winter of 1953-54."

She was a little surprised. "I never thought—" She was silent.

"Your parents were traveling there during the winter and I counted backward from your exact birth date."

She blushed. I just smiled and watched the color come to her cheeks and then go back to wherever it came from.

"I also saw a picture of your mother pregnant with you and a picture of you arriving in Indianapolis from New York when you were two weeks old."

"I was born in New York," she said, though it must have been obvious that I already knew.

"Do you know why your parents went there before you were born?"

"To get away, after my grandfather died. He died in that same summer."

I nodded. And I was realizing that in my thinking about the case I had been working mostly on whether I should take it or not. Not on how I should go about it if I did take it. Here I had my client all ready and willing to answer questions, and I didn't really know what questions I wanted to ask her.

So I thought of one.

"I need to find some people who knew your parents around the time they were married and you were born. Can you think of any who go back that far?"

She thought. "There's Mrs. Forebush. She used to be my grandfather's maid or nurse or something. Until he died. She comes over to see me sometimes and she tells me what a man my grandfather was." She made her eyes big on the word "man." "Sometimes she brings me little presents, funny things like flowers or stones or old calendars she's found. Mummy hates her. Mummy goes to her room whenever Mrs. Forebush comes around."

"What do you think of her?"

"She's OK. A little funny maybe, but she likes me."

"Is there anybody else?"

"Well, Dr. Fishman. He's my family doctor. I know he used to be my grandfather's doctor and I know he knows Mummy and Leander because he asks me about them sometimes."

I began to feel that she was tiring, but I plunged on. "Do you talk about old times with your mother?"

"Not really."

"You must have asked her things like whether she had a lot of boyfriends when she was a girl, or how she did in school. Stuff like that."

"Not really. Not a lot. That's one of the things about our family. We don't ever talk like that. The only real thing, Mummy used to take me up to the attic and read me letters she has there." She thought. "But I don't think she had real boyfriends before Leander. That's my impression."

She was pretty drained. There would be other times for other questions. Except for one. "Can you tell me what you will do with your biological father if I do find him?"

"I don't know," she said. "Maybe go and live with him. I don't know for sure."

I let it ride.

She didn't know Mrs. Forebush's address, but she gave me Dr. Fishman's. The high school she attended was Central.

My assured young woman had become a tired girl.

After she left I realized that the emotional drain and fatigue had been mutual.

5

By the time I finished dinner I had decided there were a number of ways I could go.

Mrs. Forebush looked the most direct, if she would see me. But other approaches were available.

For one thing I could try to track down some of Fleur's friends or old teachers at the Butler Nursing College. Get to the critical era by going forward from college days rather than backward from the present. The question was whether the nursing college days had been that important to Fleur Crystal.

Or I could take the general question of Eloise herself. I was fighting her fight, but the whole circumstance rested on the correctness of her blood typings.

Perhaps the thing to do was to rent a white doctor suit and go to the Crystal doorstep. "Would you all bleed into these test tubes please?"

But it wouldn't work. Eloise would giggle and blow my cover.

Instead perhaps I could learn something by talking with her teacher, Shubert, the one with whom she had done the lab work.

Or maybe Dr. Fishman would help:

From what Eloise had said about the miscarriage he knew Fleur's blood type. Certainly he would know a good deal about many of the Crystals.

Or maybe I should just go see Fleur Crystal. That would be fun. I could use all the tact of a mad elephant.

There was also a general problem of approach. But one much simpler now—after seven years in this business—than it used to be.

I called Maude Simmons. I got her permission, for ten dollars, to tell my interviewees that I was working on a feature story about the Crystals for the *Star*. If they called her to check, ten bucks more.

I decided to try Mrs. Forebush first. Having neglected to get Mrs. Forebush's first name from Eloise, I hit the phone book. Two Forebushes listed bore women's names. I tried "Anne Marie," being conservative. She was the first one listed alphabetically.

A man answered the phone. "Forebush."

I asked for Anne Marie.

"Gee, buddy, I'm sorry. She can't come to the phone; she's feeding the baby right now. But if it's about typing I can help you. She's a great little typist, she really is. Real smart. She can make a few words look like a lot or a lot of words look like a little. She was a secretary before the baby and she's real good."

I was sure she was, but she was the wrong Forebush.

A man who is alone a lot warns himself about the significance of insignificant happenings. I had picked the wrong Forebush first. Let that be a warning, I found myself telling myself. Alphabetization leads to ruin.

Florence Forebush, 413 East Fiftieth Street. Humbolt 5-8234 was the right Mrs. Forebush.

The phone call. Smallest effort clearing the biggest hurdle.

". . . and I wondered if you would be willing to help me out on this story by talking to me about the later years of your former employer, Estes Graham?"

"Estes?" Her voice was perky and light as life is long. "Why that would be very nice."

"Would tomorrow be all right?"

"Now let me see. Tomorrow is Friday. Anytime between *Let's Make a Deal* and the four-thirty movie will be just fine. Will two o'clock be all right?"

Which gave me a morning to plan for. From the legions I considered teacher Shubert, Dr. Fishman, and the nurses' college. I settled on Fishman because he should have information on more than just one person.

Wilmer Fishman, Jr., MD's phone listing gave the same number for his office and his home. I got a recording which instructed me to record a message after the chime. Instead of doing so I hung up in a mild, foolish quandry. I had expected, unconsciously, to get straight through and talk to the man. Anything else was somehow difficult.

One makes one's own problems. I hit myself on the cheek, another movement of a man alone. I called Fishman's number back again.

I left a message after the chime. Bong! Not unlike Froggie's Magic Twanger on the old *Buster Brown Show*. I would like to have a nonmedical consultation regarding one of his families. If possible tomorrow, Friday, before one o'clock. I added my name and number and hung up.

Sitting by the phone, I dwelt a moment on the contingent nature of my plans. But it was OK. If he would see me, fine. Any time left over I could use to appear unannounced at Central High School or at Butler College of Nursing. If he wouldn't see me, I could do both. Very efficient. Very businesslike. I was a finely honed machine. Hmmmmmmmmm.

I was humming.

I stopped humming, aware for the third time that my consciousness was collapsing around me. Too much alone late and soon, not enough begetting and spending.

I made one more call. To my woman. We went out for a drink. Then we came in for a drink.

6

I woke to the phone. I don't have the sense to have it by the bed—actually to have the bed by it since the cord is short. When it rings I have to scramble. It was Dr. Fishman's secretary, who said, "Please hold for Dr. Fishman." In the circumstance it seemed a very complex sentence. I mumbled and tried desperately to remember what part of the room I was in and where the clock was in this room. Success was the keynote of the day; I found the clock. It read 8:05. If the phone had been by the bed I would have taken it under the pillow.

"Mr. Samson? I believe you called."

Correct! Now leave me alone! "This is a very efficient operation you run, Doctor."

"Yes, it is." His voice was much younger than I expected. And strong. It did well at pulling me out of my dawn daze. "Just who are you, Mr. Samson?"

"I am writing an article on the family of Estes Graham, about past history and current members. I'm interviewing people who know and have known the family. I understand that you are their doctor."

"I am, and my father was before me. But what was it that you expect me to tell you?"

"I had hoped for your impressions of the family, anecdotes, anything." For openers.

"Do you have the authorization of the Crystals?"

"I haven't asked for it," you nasty man. "This is to be a feature for the Sunday *Star*. As such it's news, and it will be written anyway. So it is considered better form not to ask authorization than to ask it intending to proceed whether it is given or not."

"I see. In that case I'm afraid I shall not be able to help you. It would be bad *form* in my profession."

"I would not ask you to break any confidences," not ask, beg, "and it is not an unsympathetic article."

"Mr. Samson, short of subpoena or the specific urging of the Crystal family I shall not talk about Estes Graham, the Crystals or anything else

34

with you. Whether you are writing a story for the *Star* or for God is no concern of mine. I believe we have no further business to conduct."

The irreverent bastard. There's no accounting for people. He didn't even say good-bye.

Or good morning. I felt spiritual lack of the communion of mankind. I felt the real lack of a breakfast. Food is a major part of my life. I like it every day. But the refrigerator provided nothing to take the bitter edge off a rude awakening and a total lack of cooperation, however justifiable. I think sometimes I am not thick-skinned enough for this job.

Ahhh, well.

I munched toast and plotted.

I had chosen Fishman over Shubert and the nurses the night before, and I had chosen poorly. So I would correct myself this morning, and triumph over adversity and discombobulation.

A quarter of a loaf of toast later I set off for school.

Central is the city's "new," fancy public high school. Actually it's not in the city proper, but to the north, in Jefferson Township where most of the area's rich folks live. It has the biggest student parking lot in town.

It's not within walking distance of my office. I went down to the alley which separates my office from the City Market and picked up my zesty '58 Plymouth from its niche. Thence to Central.

At the door I was challenged by an elderly woman whose voice was weary at 9:10 in the morning. She did not look up as she spoke.

"You're late, you know. You got a pass?" She sat at a table by the door, grading papers.

"Actually, I'm right on time."

Even after she looked up there were complications. People, it seems, rarely come to the school looking for ordinary teachers. They look for principals, basketball coaches, counselors or, heaven forbid, for children.

"It's the middle of the period," she said.

"I didn't know."

She shrugged and waved me in. I looked clean. She didn't care. She was there to put late students back on the paths of righteousness.

Prowling around the lobby I found a room labeled "Faculty Lounge." I went in without knocking. Where better to find faculty? Inside it looked like a classroom with its dirty student desks arranged in rows. I could tell the improvement in educational methods immediately. In my day desks were bolted to the floor.

Here men and women sat smoking in the corners and there was a coffee machine in front where one might expect a gesticulating teacher. I approached a pert, mini-skirted brunette with strands of blond carefully located in her flowing hair. She was pushing three buttons on the machine simultaneously. Coffee Black. Extra Cream. Extra Sugar.

"It's the only way to get cream and sugar on this machine," she said. "Are you a sub? I bet you're looking for the cigarette machine. We don't have one. The superintendent had them removed when the cancer stuff came out. I'd give you one of mine only I only have two left and most men don't like menthol anyway." She looked up at me as if it were now my turn.

"I was hoping to find a teacher here. Mr. Shubert. A biology teacher."

"Oh, Johnny. The married one. He isn't free until third. That'll be after the rest of second and home room."

"About what time will that be?"

"You're not a sub then, are you?"

"No. I'm not."

"Um. Too bad," she said, trying to be enigmatic. Presumably she only put out in the profession. "Home room ends in about half an hour. He should be in then. He isn't old enough to go anywhere else and he's not one of those intellectual freaky types."

"Good," I said, not understanding the hurdles I had surmounted.

She picked up her coffee, until then cooling in the machine's pocket, and she carried it into a group, all men, in the back of the room.

Which left me with the morning *Star*, sitting in the Central High School Faculty Lounge.

In the forty minutes before John Shubert made his entrance, people came and people left, but not a soul spoke a word to me.

No. That is not exactly correct. Twenty-five minutes after I sat down, as if knowing I was stuck on "soak" in three letters, a speaker in the ceiling came alive. A chime was struck. A deep resonant voice, marred

36

only by the heavy nasal hangover of rural Hoosier speech, greeted us boys and girls and instructed us to rise for the Pledge to the flag. The teachers in the lounge did not move a muscle. They were either conscious of not having been addressed, or just insensate to everything that was going on around them. But whatever it was, it was OK by me. I didn't feel much like getting up.

A recording of the "Star-Spangled Banner" followed the Pledge, and the singing was led by a live, bass, hick voice.

The music stopped, but the voice did not. "That recording of our national anthem and many other fine tunes can be bought on the Central High School Band recording which is now available in each and every home room from your band-recording representative. Support your band and help get them new instruments. Only five bucks apiece. Buy two and give them as gifts." The day's announcements concluded with the ringing of a chime. Home room over. There was a flurry of exits and entrances in the Faculty Lounge.

I recognized John Shubert by the biology book stuffed with papers which he carried. And because he looked married.

"Shit," he announced to the lounge in general and no one in particular. "There has got to be a better way to make a living."

"Dedication, John, dedication," scolded a healthy-looking man who was crammed into a student-size desk. He shuffled a pack of cards. I approached them.

"Mr. Shubert? I would very much like to speak with you about one of your students."

"Do you mind talking over cards? This is my gin period. The closest I can get in this place." He sat down in one of the desks and, driving it like a bump-em car, turned it around to face the shuffler, who now dealt. I squeezed into the desk across the aisle from Shubert. He nodded to his friend. "This is Clark Mace. Who do you want to know about?"

"An Eloise Crystal." The cardsharp dealt slowly and with great concentration, as if wanting to make no mistakes.

"Aah, Eloise Crystal." Shubert rocked back in his seat, as all the things I wanted to know came into his mind. "May I ask who you are?"

"My name is Albert Samson. I am a personnel investigator for Eli Lilly. We have a Saturday science program which Eloise Crystal has applied for a place in. There are a number of high school applicants and

37

I am checking with their science teachers to get some idea of what they are like."

"Isn't it usual to send a form?"

"Would you really rather we sent a form?"

"Amen, brother," interjected the patient dealer.

"A job requiring some science," said Shubert, savoring the idea. I thought it was a pretty good one. "That's a surprise."

"Why?"

"She has never given me much indication that she is, well, career-oriented. To be perfectly frank, I'm more surprised that she is applying for a job than that it involves science. What sort of stuff is she supposed to do?"

"We will be training in laboratory skills. It's a matter of aptitude mostly, but a little biology would help. She mentioned that she has done some extra laboratory work with you. Blood typing, I believe."

"Ah, the blood typing. She's very good at it too. She has quite a taste for genetics. Hasn't missed a day since we started it. Genetics has a lot bigger part in the course these days, you know. DNA and all that. We start on it early in the course and use it to develop ecology and natural selection. It's a little unusual to do it that way. We're quite proud."

"Do you consider her a bright girl?"

"Definitely bright, but a little distracted sometimes. What strikes her fancy she is extremely good at. Things stick in her mind; she does extra work. What doesn't strike her goes through like a sieve, or more often she just doesn't come to school."

"Doesn't come to school?"

"Oh, I guess she just hangs around. What do any of them do?" He cocked his head. "Say, are you sure *she* applied for the job? Are you sure that her father didn't apply for her? He set it up, am I right?"

"Her father is involved in it."

"I thought so. He came in to see me recently. He seemed genuinely concerned about her. An only child, I believe. Apparently she has become difficult at home. Seemed a nice enough type."

"I'm afraid I haven't met him yet." I was laying it on just a little bit thick. "Well, thank you very much, Mr. Shubert. I won't take any more of your time."

He waved his neglected cards magnanimously.

"I would appreciate it if you would not mention my speaking to you to Eloise. I suspect it would just make her nervous on the final qualification tests."

He nodded. "For her sake I hope she gets it."

"We'll give her every consideration."

Pleased with the apparent success of my little deception, I left the Faculty Lounge. Certain priority things had been accomplished. A degree of support for Eloise's rationality; a degree of confirmation for the blood types. It was about a quarter after ten and I had plenty of time. No one was visible in the school lobby now. The main door was closed, the table abandoned.

A tight-run little ship. No need for guards. Suppressing an impulse to go to the general office and purchase a nickel's worth of band tunes for five bucks I strode quietly and reasonably happily to my car.

How can a self-respecting cop put a parking ticket on a '58 Plymouth? Is there no respect for age in this country? I whipped it off the windshield and then really got burned. It wasn't even a real ticket.

> It is against school regulations to park in a faculty space without an identifying sticker. Please do not do so again. Your license number has been recorded. If this is not your first offense you will be reported to the Police Department which will issue a parking violation.

Schools, I love em! So I headed off for another one.

I came into Butler on Forty-ninth Street. Past the two Butler University landmarks I was familiar with. Butler Fieldhouse, which is called Hinkle Fieldhouse now. They play basketball there. Very nice.

Then past a body of water known unto me as Stagnation Pond. In my day it was a lush little pool; water came in, water went out. Clear fresh water that grew pretty flowers in the summer and made good ice skating in the winter. I used to go there with my friends when I was in high school. Lots of people used to go there. But no longer. Poor pool. Stinks all summer and even the winter ice is lumpy from the stuff that grows in it.

When I got to center campus, I just followed the signs to the Nursing College. I had never been there before, proof positive that I had gone to college outside Indiana.

By a few minutes after eleven I had located the registrar's office and entered it.

I don't know if she was the registrar, but the only person I saw behind a long counter was a one-armed lady in civilian clothes. I did something of a double take; one does not see many one-armed ladies in this world. It's a reflection on our role divisions.

I approached her end of the counter as she approached mine.

"Yeah? What can I do for ya?"

"I hate to be troublesome," I lied, "but a woman who used to go to this college has applied to my company for a job and we still haven't gotten her transcripts from you."

"Oh, yeah?" She peered; she pursed her mouth; she shrugged. "What's the name and the class?"

"She never graduated, but she started in 1949. The name is Fleur Graham."

From the counter she went to some filing cabinets and surprisingly quickly she returned with the academic record of Fleur Graham.

I glanced over it. It gave little information. Name; home address; campus address (same); the name of her high school; her birth date; and the list of the courses she had taken in her one and only year. The grades were all recorded as "inc" for incomplete. A fine record. I had one like that once, the first semester of my sophomore year of the first time I went to college.

"Is there any way I can find out if any of her teachers are still teaching here?"

"Gee. We ain't got records of the teachers of the courses she took, mister. Teachers come and teachers go."

"Well. Can I have a copy of this transcript, then?"

"Yeah, sure." She took it and made a Xerox copy. "That'll be a dime."

Which I paid her, and left.

The transcript was not entirely helpful, but it had served to cut out any possibility of the one thing I had been hoping for from Butler. Friends of Fleur's from her nursing days. The lady had lived at home, not in the residential halls. The best I could do now would be to try to

40

contact all the other girls who started Butler Nursing College in 1949 and ask them if they happened to remember anything about a quiet girl called Fleur who might have been in some of their classes. Not a very efficient process. Not to waste time on now.

From the Nursing College I went back to center campus and parked. I had about an hour and a half before I was due at Mrs. Forebush's so I decided to take it over a leisurely lunch. I looked around for a university cafeteria. It's easy enough to eat in ostensibly private dining halls if they are large. You just walk in frowning. That makes it seem as if you belong there because you know what the food is going to be like.

The food was not good, but at least there was not a lot of it. I dawdled over coffee and eavesdropped on nearby conversations as best I could.

Then a couple of tootsies came over and tried to make friends. We talked for fully twenty minutes about how hard our courses were. Mine won. Nursing can be very hard on "an older fella." They were very sympathetic and were a bit surprised when, at a quarter of two, I took my leave.

7

At 2:05 I pulled up in front of 413 East Fiftieth Street. It was a barn-red house, frame with barn-red trim. A small, heavily planted garden filled the small front yard. A driveway led behind the house from Fiftieth Street on the left, and an alley ran beside it on the right.

My fist was raised to knock when the door opened.

"Come in, come in," said the trim white-haired lady with a yellow carnation in her hair. Florence Forebush.

I came in and was led into what they used to call a drawing room. It was frilly, Victorian and full of violet-brown upholstery with white lace trim. Two chairs and a couch were horseshoed in front of a large marble

41

fireplace which bore a mantel loaded with pictures. Some of them I recognized. Three, the different ages of Estes Graham. A woman next to him. The print and frame looked old. It was Irene Olian Graham, I was sure. Next to her the uniformed figure of Leander Crystal. On the end the most familiar face. My client's.

I apologized for being late.

"It's a little early yet for tea, Mr. Samson," said Mrs. Forebush after we had seated ourselves in the matching chairs and faced each other across a slate coffee table. Her decorum contrasted with a social omission on her mantel. No Fleur.

"You'll have to remind me what it was you wanted again. About Estes?"

"That's right, Mrs. Forebush. I'm trying to get together some information about Estes Graham and his family."

"For the paper, I believe you said? About Estes' last years?"

What was I supposed to have reminded her of again? She had repeated everything I had told her. I was getting the distinct impression that I was being conned, not conning. But maybe I was just touchy. "I hope so, yes."

She studied me quizzically. "I trust you won't mind me saying this so directly, but you look a little old not to be sure when you are doing something."

Challenged again. "I hope not to make that your problem. I just understood you knew Estes Graham in his later years."

She shrugged. "Oh, I'm happy enough to talk about Estes. Nothing I can say will matter to him now."

Was she really telling me that she didn't believe the whole story?

"I worked for Estes Graham from my twenty-first birthday until the day he died. I saw that man go through more than a dozen lesser men together could take." Light seemed to come from her eyes, rather than from the window. She *was* happy enough to talk about Estes Graham.

"I understand he married Irene Olian."

"In 1916. The quietest, most angelic little girl you ever saw. He worshiped her. He mostly died himself when she was taken in 1937."

"There were four children?"

"Three boys dead in the war, and a girl, Fleur. Young man, as far as I'm concerned, there is more story in Estes Graham than there will ever be in one man again. Things just aren't the same for a real man

42

nowadays. But his last years, they were such a change. Now why do you want to hear about that?" She looked me straight in the eye. But she out-eyed me, three to two. The yellow carnation watching dispassionately down from above.

I said, "That's the part of the story I'm supposed to cover for the article."

Her snort covered what would have been my choking on my own feeble words.

"Goodness gracious. A man your age 'hoping' to do a story and now it's not even all your story." She snorted again, with no apologies. I had the distinct impression I was not smart enough to dabble in private eying. Maybe I should stick to writing crossword puzzles.

She brought me up short again. "Young man, you aren't doing anything that might hurt the child, are you?"

I knew she meant Eloise.

"No, Mrs. Forebush. I am trying to help her. It was she who gave me your name."

"Eloise," she mused. She sat back in her chair, the body equivalent of clearing her throat. "All right. You must think I can tell you things you need to know. I'll do my best."

"Thank you," I said, infinitely grateful.

She looked at her watch. "Still, you must get on with it. I don't want to miss my movie."

"It shouldn't take that long, Mrs. Forebush. I need to know about Fleur Crystal."

"Dreadful child. On the surface so meek and mild, but underneath she's just a little conniver. I guess it was the war that really did it, losing all three boys, and so soon after Irene. She spent every minute of her life trying to make her father love her."

"And he didn't?"

"Just the minimum. A little mouse like her. He liked women to have some style. Fleur always whined." Then she added quietly, "Irene had style. It didn't have to be brash."

"Fleur was devoted to him?"

"Utterly."

"But not so much as not to get married."

"That was as much to please her father as anything, you know. But he's nice, that Mr. Crystal. I fail to see what he saw in her."

43

"If not woman, maybe money?"

"Oh, no. He's just not that way. Do you know that the day after Estes died Mr. Crystal came straight to me, gave me this house, and started sending me money every month? He didn't need to do that. I told him that Estes made arrangements for me before he died, but Mr. Crystal still keeps sending me living money. He told me to keep the other for savings. So I've fixed the place up. Took out all the tall shrubs that were here when I came. Put in plants of my own.

"But I'm getting off the track. My two best subjects are my house and the old days. You'll have to guide me to the material that you want."

"You were talking about Fleur marrying Leander Crystal."

"Yes. He was a friend of Joshua's, you know. Baby Joshua's. They knew each other in the war and Mr. Crystal came to us after it was all over and told us about it. It was so sad."

"What was, Mrs. Forebush?"

"The way poor Joshie died. I mean after the real war was all over. He died in France when a truck exploded. Mr. Crystal was there and heard his last words, love to his father, and his brothers and his sister and to me. It makes me teary even now, to think of it. I cried for days then. We all did. He didn't even know that his brothers were dead."

Spontaneously we paused in silence. So much more meaningful than any routine pledge can be.

"But I must say, Mr. Crystal took to little Fleur from the beginning. He tried to help Estes put a little purpose in her. I think he was as responsible as anyone for getting Fleur to try nursing. Did you know she studied nursing?"

I nodded. She continued.

"But of course she just wasn't up to self-discipline. They got married at the end of a summer, 1949 it was."

"How did the marriage seem to affect her?"

"She was better for a while. Gayer. After the marriage it took Fleur some time to realize that Estes was really looking to her for grandchildren. She thought that when she and Mr. Crystal were married, her father would just come around to her. It didn't work out that way. It made her real nervous about having children. She went to doctors and finally Mr. Crystal took her to Europe. He thought it might be good for them. And when they got back she was pregnant, sure enough, with Eloise. Made Estes real happy. He didn't believe a marriage was

44

approved by God until there were children. I really think he would have liked Eloise.

"How is she, Mr. Samson? I haven't seen her in quite a while."

"I think she is fine, Mrs. Forebush. A real young lady. But I must ask you a frank question, about Eloise's mother."

"OK. Shoot."

"Is there any chance in your mind that she could be unfaithful?" Mrs. Forebush tried hard to fathom the significance of the question, and then fell back on her resolve to help. "Well, I haven't talked to the girl for years. I can't say what she might be capable of."

"I don't mean now, Mrs. Forebush. I mean then. Those first years of marriage, through the time of Estes Graham's death."

Her answer was absolute by human measure. "Not a chance in a million."

That had been the big question, so we rapidly prepared for my departure.

She said, "I really don't know what this is all about, Mr. Samson. One loses one's faculties. But you will tell Eloise to come and see me. I think that'd be better than my going to see her right now."

"I'll do that."

"And you, Mr. Samson. You must come again and tell me exactly what is going on."

It was not a request. It was a threat. "I shall, Mrs. Forebush."

"Thank you, Mr. Samson. Now, good-bye."

I walked slowly down the walk to my car. She was an unusual lady. Vibrant and on top of things. I liked her, and although I had come into her house telling lies, I believed that she liked me.

I sat for a few minutes in the car making notes on what she had told me. Most immediately relevant was her exclusion of any chance that Fleur had had an extramarital love life. Especially considering the facts.

While I sat I happened to look up and catch the eye of an old man sitting on the porch of the house across the alley from Mrs. Forebush's. It made me nervous. I couldn't tell if he knew I was looking at him or not. How do you tell whether somebody is seeing what is in front of him?

I started the car, and just before easing the stick into first I made half a wave. He made no response at all. But on the other hand my gesture was not definitive enough to prove anything one way or the other.

For all he knew I could have been failing to catch a mosquito.
He didn't move for as long as I saw him.

I headed in the general direction of home. But as I hadn't finished my notes I stopped at a drugstore for some coffee.

Once inside and working I remembered I had not eaten much of my lunch. That made me feel peckish.

And after I ordered meat replica on a bun I got into a conversation with the grill man about whether the Pacers could do it again. They had played their first game of the season while I was jollying last night. They'd had their own jollies at half time. A bomb scare had emptied the Coliseum. But no boom and the Pacers had proceeded to lower the boom on Kentucky.

It was about four fifteen before I got started again, back to the office.

8

When I got back to the office, I had a surprise waiting for me in her chair. Eloise Crystal, client. My outside office door has no lock, except for a bolt when I'm inside. It's one of the ways my slumlord tries to get me to move to the suite next door. I just keep the room to my inner life secured and try to leave nothing of value in the office. It's more friendly that way. Clients have a place to rest their beleaguered bones when they show up and their ever-workin' PI ain't home.

She smiled as I came in. For some reason that touched me. You get so little that is personal, human in this business. Either you are serving legal papers to unsuspecting merchants or your client is trying to get you to seduce his wife so he can charge adultery. Her smile made me feel good.

"I didn't know whether I should come today," she said. "You didn't say."

"I guess I forgot. It's nice to see you. I hope it wasn't trouble."

"The only thing was that I didn't know whether you were coming back or not. It's nearly five. I have to go at five."

By this time I was sitting on my side of the desk, feeling rather

46

relaxed. Inappropriately so, perhaps, but it was the first conversation I'd had all day with someone I was not trying to con.

"How do you get around?" I asked. "By bus all the time?"

"Oh, no. Sometimes by cab. Sometimes I even walk."

I smiled a little embarrassedly. I was making small talk, but had implicitly been attacking her age again. In this city kids who are really sixteen have drivers' licenses. It wasn't her fault she'd paid me to find out her real age.

I think she realized what I was thinking. She said, "Is it important?"

I said, "No."

"Well, I know something about you too. I know that you've only been in Indianapolis for seven years and that you're not crooked."

"Oh?"

"I called the Better Business Bureau. They haven't had any complaints on you."

I grinned.

"I called before I came the first time. I picked your name out of the yellow pages because all you had in it was your name. Nothing about 'marital investigations' or stuff like that. Then I called to find out if you were crooked."

Before me was a girl who could get blood out of her environmental father.

"Maybe I'm just too small to specialize, and so crooked that I pay them off." I tried to look crooked.

"Oh, I don't think so." She smiled again. We smiled at each other. I began to get uncomfortable. I am not accustomed to confidence freely offered. It made me realized that I had not been very aggressive about getting information that would be of use to her. I mean, how much use was the knowledge that her mother got incompletes in nursing school?

For the moment I bore the guilt of the ungrateful employee.

I decided to give her a chance to assuage my sensitivities.

"I don't have a lot I can tell you today," I said.

She didn't assuage. "Haven't you at least checked my blood typings yet?"

"Not yet," I said. "Only indirectly."

She continued nipping at my heels. Hound and hare. "But isn't that the first thing you have to do? To make sure that I'm not, well, that I'm not just crazy or something."

47

To make sure that I was not just the kid's equivalent of a hypochondriac's doctor.

"It's not all that easy a thing to check," I said.

"Didn't you see Dr. Fishman?"

"He wouldn't talk to me."

"But he's so nice!" Maybe to rich girls. "Why didn't he talk to you?"

"He said nothing he knows is any of my business. I could hardly tell him what my real business is."

"I guess not," she said. "Still . . ."

I knew she was disappointed. She had realized that little things could stop me. That I would take no for an answer.

I was a little disappointed myself.

For self-protection I said, "You can't expect this to go fast. It's a difficult problem." It sounded flimsy even to me.

"I know," she said. "It's just that I've been thinking so much. It's just that I'd hoped—" She paused because we both knew what she'd hoped. Forty-eight-hour service. "Can you tell me what you have done?"

"I talked to your biology teacher, to the registrar of the Butler Nursing College, and to Mrs. Forebush. I think I have a better idea of what your mother and your grandfather are like. Were like."

"I never knew him."

"I know. His time ended before yours began."

"My mother still thinks about him a lot. Sometimes she accidentally calls Leander Daddy. A mistake like, you know? Leander hates it."

"Does it bother you?" Not the world's least ambiguous question, but a proper grunt to keep her talking.

"I'm sort of used to it. To her. When she isn't unhappy we get along OK. When I was little we used to play out where she used to play with her brothers. But since she had the miscarriage she's been miserable and when she's unhappy it's awful. She thinks she's dying, and it's too bad because she was so happy while she was pregnant."

"Why?"

"I guess just being pregnant and going to have babies." A cunning look came over my client's face. "Say, you don't think my real father has been around, do you?"

I shrugged. "What do you think about my talking to your mother?"

"Talking about what?"

48

"I'm not quite at the point of asking her what we want to know, but it might help in indirect ways."

"You can tell her you are the truant officer. I cut school a lot." I suppose it's the modern thing to do.

"When time comes I'll work out something that will keep me out of trouble."

"Are you afraid of trouble?"

"Yes, definitely." No, not really. I just don't go looking for it unless there is a reason.

"I didn't think private detectives were supposed to be like that."

Which I responded to by facial expression only.

"I'm being childish, aren't I?"

"Yes."

"I have to go home now anyway. I was being childish with you to prepare for my role at home." She stood up. "I think the money I gave you runs out tomorrow. Here's some more. I saw my trust man at the bank and told him I needed a new winter outfit."

I reached forward and took the envelope she proffered and put it on the desk. "Thanks," I said.

"Don't you want to look and see how much there is?"

"I'm sure there is enough for me to get a new winter outfit."

"I guess."

"We need a way that I can get in touch with you so you don't have to come here every day."

"I don't mind coming here."

"It's just that I don't always get back here by five."

"Oh, I don't mind. I can just sit and think of all the good things you are finding out for me."

"We'll see."

"OK. Bye."

And she byed.

While the cuckoo counted the fingers on one of its wings, I opened the envelope and counted out ten hundred-dollar bills. At thirty-five plus, that made for a fair stretch of employment. An amazing girl, my child client. I was learning a little more about her every day.

For instance, that of the two of us, she was the more spontaneously aggressive. Not that I cannot be aggressive, but I tend to hold back unless there is something very specific that I want. That's why she had made me feel bad about Wilmer Fishman, Jr., MD. She made me realize that he had some specific things that I wanted.

The early hour I'd talked to him was my excuse. I gathered my belongings and visited my inner chamber. At a few minutes after five, the morning seemed a long, long time ago.

I gathered some equipment, divested myself of identification, and stuffed my winter outfit into my back pocket. And went home to eat.

9

Bud's Dugout is where it's been for about seventeen years, out a little on Virginia Avenue. Past the railroad tracks. Southeast Indianapolis. Prices are up but Ma keeps the menu pretty constant. The pinball machines are about the only things that are changed regularly. She has four, and one gets replaced every three or four months. They wear out, you know, especially when they get a lot of action. They can be adjusted for a while, but it takes more and more servicing and they lose their liveliness. That's sad in a good machine. But humans seem to make their machines with the same inherent sadnesses they have themselves.

"Hello, boy," she said when she looked up and saw me sitting at the counter. She had only a couple of customers when I came in, so I stayed in the front. When it's crowded I go to the back. Like me, she used to have a separate apartment, but when Bud finally died she moved into the back of the Dugout. Bud was my father.

"How's the baby? You hear from her recently?" She was asking after her granddaughter.

"I haven't heard in the last week or two, but I sent her a note."

"When are you going to see her next?" She passed me a bowl of her chili. And tea, real pot-brewed tea.

"Not sure, Ma. Soon maybe." I come around every few weeks, to check up on her. See she's OK. We're not close, exactly, but we're not far either. Tonight she was doing pretty well, well enough. Tired but unbowed. She owns the place, not a mortgage. I paid that off back the one time I was doing well.

Two people came in, a young couple. They picked a table, then conferred a moment. The girl went to play Hayride, while the boy came to the counter to wait for Ma. He ordered cheeseburgers and french fries, and then he joined the girl. They each played one flipper.

Ma bent over and whispered in my ear. "They like the machines. What do you think they do?"

I looked, but could get no clues from clothes. While I watched, they missed a replay and traded flippers. I shrugged and shook my head.

"Teachers!" Ma looked smug and I could see why. They were so young! "*She* told me," Ma continued. "They teach high school. He teaches math at Tech; she teaches French and Latin in some private school. I forget the name."

I shrugged and shook my head. I had had my schools for the day. It reminded me of business. I took the one thousand dollars from my hip pocket and passed it to my mother. "Keep this for me, will you?"

She looked in the envelope. "What for?"

"Bail maybe. I got it too late to put in the bank, and it isn't safe to carry." She knew I meant—not safe if I was arrested.

"You expect trouble?"

"No, but it can't hurt to be prepared." The young couple cooed and chortled. They had won a free game.

"All right, boy. Take care though."

"I will, Ma." I don't often go to Ma's just to eat, but when I do I get the strange feeling of being like a cop. I leave without paying.

10

The Fishman Clinic turned out to be a modern, rather small one-story building on Route 100 near the Nora Shopping Center. Nora is now just part of the sprawling north-side suburbs of Indianapolis.

I drove past the clinic going west and turned into the shopping center.

At night the problem was not to get a parking space, but to get one in the midst of enough cars that mine would not be left unshielded when the stores started closing. If I was delayed too long inside, my car would be sitting naked on the field of asphalt. Patrol cops are suspicious of that, especially if they have been on the patrol for a while and know which cars belong to shop staff. Cops get promotion brownie points for their arrests. I very much preferred not to become the night's brownie point. Although getting caught would not be disastrous. I do have some friends who can get me out of small-time trouble. It's just life is so much easier if you don't get caught at your illegal doings. Cops—except the few I know fairly well, like Jerry Miller who I went to high school with—are just strangers carrying guns.

And I don't like guns. I don't carry them.

I shot a man once while I was working for the Tomgrove Security Company in 1957. It was near the end of my tether with them—I spent three and a half years—and I was still young and foolish. They told me to carry a gun, so I did.

I was assigned to catch a man who had been pilfering things at night from a construction site. When I did, he smacked me in the face with a board. Only not hard enough because it didn't knock me out. So I plugged him. Not dead, but just dead enough to kill something in me.

Of the various stores in the Nora Shopping Center I decided the drugstore was the most likely to stay open late. I waited ten minutes just to get a space right in front of it. When I had parked, I took the equipment out of the car. Camera, electronic flash, gloves, penlight, a few simple picks and my little tripod stool with a string on it. I walked through the parking lot's shadows to the nearby clinic.

I headed for the back. I was fairly confident. It was not the type of clinic I figured would do a large business with addicts of various sorts, so probably it didn't keep any sizable store of exciting drugs.

The key was the kind of security arrangements Fishman felt appropriate. My knowledge of alarms was solid, but a little out-of-date. I knew them pretty well when I was a security man, but if he was one of those device-oriented suburban doctors, I was in trouble.

As I waxed cowardly, I examined the windows on the back side of the building. I picked what I thought was a bathroom window—higher than the others.

I had one thing going for me, the place had lots of windows. The installation cost of covering them all electrically, plus doors and cabinets, would be huge. I just hoped Fishman hadn't had lots of money when he built the joint. All I needed now was a doctor in business for his health.

I opened the tripod stool underneath the high window. I took the free end of the string tied to its leg and I attached it to my belt. I examined the window with my penlight. I saw no traces of devices. I went at it.

One of my picks and a little muscle slipped the window catch. I was inside. I pulled the stool up to the window ledge by its string and carefully knocked off the dirt clinging to its legs. Then I brought it inside.

If I had tripped an alarm, it was silent. I closed the window. A quick pan with the penlight showed me the details of a women's rest room. Not my first visit to such a place. I found the door and tried it. It was locked. He locked the ladies'. Wonderment set in, as I worked at the lock. Maybe it was a good omen. Maybe he was a locker, and not a bugger.

I stepped into the hall and looked around. Within a few minutes I found the receptionist's office. I went in. I was looking for files but I didn't find them.

Two doors led out of the room. Both locked. Soon both unlocked. One was the doctor's office. In the other I found the files.

A special file room, accessible from both the doctor's and receptionist's offices. There was a bank of filing cabinets in the middle of the room. They were on a rotating base, so with a little effort you could get to the fronts of four sides of files. Very modern.

I hesitated before I started on the file cabinet's locks. This might be the biggest gamble so far. If, by some chance, special papers or drugs were kept in the room, the odds of electric reprisals were considerable. My time would be short. So before I started on them I prepared my camera in case a few seconds would make a difference.

Most detectives who photograph records have special equipment for it. I don't get much call for industrial spying, so I have to make do with the equipment I have. The electronic flash, for instance, is prohibitively bright for this sort of close-up work. Rather than get another I have rigged a filter for the flash which cuts out about 70 percent of the light. Makes it more suitable for close-ups. I also use a relatively slow film.

I opened the files. As far as I knew I had triggered no alarms.

Busy hands are tools of the Lord. I located "Crystal" in the front file. There was a folder for each of them. Fleur, Leander, and Eloise. I took them out one by one. Spread the sheets on the floor and took pictures of each side of each pair of pages.

After finishing the three Crystals I checked the file for Graham and found nothing. That disturbed me momentarily. I was interested in Estes Graham's medical history, so I started checking the contents of the various trays in the rest of the cabinets. Visions of a separate file or an archives room or microfilmed records flitted through my mind. But when I had rotated the bank of files to bring its back to front I found an entire cabinet marked "Wilmer Fishman, Sr.," and from these I extracted files on six Grahams. A husband, a wife and four children. The pages were densely covered and the decaying paper made for poorer contrast. I prayed for legible pictures and snapped away. One by one, side by side.

By the end I was sweating and my batteries were taking longer and longer to get up the oomph for a flash. They had had a rough night.

I paused after my last Graham, only to think if there was anyone else I wanted information on. I looked under Olian and found nothing. I was glad, and more quickly than I had opened them, I closed the files and relocked their trays.

My next problem was getting out. I contemplated retracing my steps. The conservative exit. But slipping out the ladies' room window didn't appeal to me. I felt too good for that. Too successful. I was swept by a premature feeling of elation. I chose the honorable way out. I left by the front door. When I finally found it.

It was latched. Two latches, one door. He was a locker. I saw no wires or other danger signs. I was in a hurry to be out of there, to be home. I threw the latches, and stepped out the door.

On the top step I looked briefly into the sky. A clear, fall night. It felt cool, because of the moisture still beaded on my forehead. Cool and good. It felt clean. I felt springy. I felt I belonged on a top step.

To add an elegant touch for unpresent eyes I turned to the door and made as if to lock it.

I was flooded by light.

I froze. The light stayed on me. React! Think fast!

"Charlie?" I asked, turning, bluffing, knees shaking.

"No," said the voice. "This is Eddie."

"Well, good night, Eddie," I said and tripped down the steps, toward the light. It stayed on me for a moment and then dropped, illuminating the sidewalk in front of me.

"Good night, sir," the voice said. Recognizably old. More recognizable than that. Generic voice of the aging security guard. Bless him.

I turned into the empty parking lot at the right end of the clinic. I walked as surely as I could. I was still shaking but I had made it.

I glanced back and saw Eddie continuing on his rounds. Probably hired by the shopping center and paid extra by Fishman to extend his patrol. My look back took in part of the back of the clinic. I had an impulse to run back and wipe out the marks the stool must have made in the dirt below the window. My only incriminating marks.

I controlled myself. Foolish consistency is the hobgoblin of little minds. Tonight I had a big mind. I was back at the car, almost home free. Despite my precautions it stood alone in the lot. But I didn't care. I would let the marks be. I just wanted to get out. Get away. Who could prove that the marks were left by my stool?

My stool.

I did not have my stool.

I collapsed on the front right fender. In my mind, I could see the stool sitting by the wall in the file room. Plain as it could be. I had walked right by it on my way out.

On the very long drive home I had to pull over to the curb twice. My knees and hands were shaking so much I could not get them to drive.

I did make it home and up the stairs. By that time the self-protecting forces had begun to exert themselves in my mind. There were no identifiable markings on the stool, and I had left nothing which characterized me uniquely. No fingerprints. Probably Eddie wouldn't be able to recognize me again; probably he hadn't even noticed the camera on its strap by my side. Fishman, at the worst, would suspect me by association and warn Leander. But warn him of what? Someone asking questions about the family for some article? I hadn't given him Maude's name. He had no details except my name. He could find out I am a PI and what then?

The notion intrigued me a little—it might be interesting to see if anything did come of it all. Leander Crystal had not occupied much of my attention. He certainly was relevant, present at the scene. As close to the scene as I had got so far.

Would he think Fleur was starting divorce action? What *could* he think?

And, for it all, I was at home now and not arrested or otherwise interfered with. I had obtained film with the information I wanted. The only task was to obtain the information from the film.

I set about developing it.

When I first started working with photographic equipment I would have had to take this film to be professionally developed. Developing film, especially if it is important not to damage any part of it, is a fairly difficult business. But I'm pretty good at it now. With a routine established over the years I get pretty good negatives.

My big decision was whether to let the film dry overnight or try to rush it to get the prints right away. But that would have made waiting for the prints to dry a thing too. I would want to start reading them.

I decided to let the films dry in peace overnight. I hung them up in my closet *cum* darkroom. And then I hung myself out to dry; still shaking. I watched a late movie. Or two.

11

I woke up at seven thirty. Much too early, but I couldn't fall back asleep and after a few seconds of consciousness, I didn't want to.

In my own terms I had risked a good deal for the pictures I'd taken, and I wanted to find out what was on them. The only question was whether I should print them before or after breakfast.

I printed them before breakfast.

Since I was on an expense account, I decided to be thorough. I printed two eight-by-ten copies of each medical file page. I quick-fixed and quick-washed them. I put one set of ferrotype tins in the oven for a quick dry. The others I left loose on towels around the room. I made some morning coffee.

The prints in the oven dried fast, all right, but rolled up into little cylinders. I had to flatten them all over the edge of the table. That done, I sorted them out, and took a look at the fruits of my labor.

First things first. I tried Fleur's current file.

56

It turns out that a doctor's record is not the easiest thing in the world to read. It meant very little to me.

Finally I managed to interpret dates. Like, the record was opened on July 21, 1956, not with a visit, but with a note which read "Sr.-7/21/56." I took a guess that it meant she had been Fishman, Senior's, patient and had been taken over on that date by the son. Presumably on the elder Fishman's retirement or demise.

There was a section titled "history." I couldn't read it.

The pages of appointments I could read. There weren't any.

I began to wonder if I was missing something. Maybe there was some gap in my education. All it meant to me was that Fleur had not seen Dr. Fishman since 1956. Why should that be peculiar? I told me why. Because he was supposed to be the family doctor. So I had to be missing something.

Like what happened about the miscarriage.

I poured a cup of coffee and collated Leander Crystal's medical file. Marked "Sr.-7/21/56." With much less history space filled in, equally illegible. I passed on to appointments.

Empty, like Fleur's.

Dummy files? Dummy detective?

Or healthy Crystals? When one has risked more than one cares to lose, it is depressing to find that you have won very little. Information doesn't become more valuable just because it was hard to get.

More coffee.

I took the current file for Eloise Crystal. Dated 11/17/54, some two weeks after her birth, the day after her arrival in Indianapolis. I presumed that Fishman, Junior, had been her doctor from the beginning. Or rather from her first appearance in Indianapolis.

Appointments galore. Nearly sixteen years worth. Miscellaneous words I could make out.

But even the full file depressed me. Because I figured if I spent a lot of time I could work out most of it, but I wouldn't have any way of knowing ahead of time whether there would be anything important. It was the inefficiency which appalled me.

After a dreadful, eventful, exciting day yesterday, and not enough sleep. Especially not enough sleep.

I went to the old files of Wilmer Fishman, Senior. I started with Fleur's again. No blank here, but I was too low to absorb much.

File opened, presumably at birth, on June 9, 1930. Particularly dense from the late 1930's on.

At least I knew now who had paid for the Fishman Clinic: Estes Graham.

Leander first visited Fishman in 1947. I assumed that he had been referred by Estes. He had made sporadic visits, roughly two a year, until 1953. The last listed appointment was January 5, 1953. Then nothing. For seventeen years. Money cures many ills, but that was ridiculous.

I took up Fleur's three brothers. Windom, the eldest, Sellman, then Joshua. Last appointments for each in the early forties. The three heroes, dead. "Deceased" was marked at the bottom of each file.

Irene Olian Graham's was short. She had died in 1937. I had my first look into a doctor's view of a patient who had died under his care. Under the last appointment was the notation. "Deceased 2/19/37. 156201."

I realized after only a few minutes that the number was not likely to be the number of patients who had died on Dr. Fishman, Sr. Perhaps a certificate number, for the corpse.

The last appointment bore the same date and I found a notation that looked very much like "hv." I decided that it was probably meant to be "hv," for house visit. Thank you, dear Watson. I had another cup of coffee.

I leafed back through Fleur's records. There were what appeared to be literally a hundred house visits in the older file. Fleur, I realized, made me uncomfortable. The cumulative effect of the things I had found out, or hadn't found out. I felt less and less sure of ever knowing her, but surer that someday I would be meeting her. I was depressed.

Estes Graham. First ministered to by Fishman, Senior, in what appeared to be 1901. Senior could not have been much more than just starting in practice then. And who knew what Estes was starting. His visits had been infrequent, years apart at times, until 1946 when they had become regular and frequent. Many notes and symbols and numbers.

I concentrated furiously, but I could not find any familiar words. My loathing of television doctor programs had served me ill. Clearly there had been a major change in the state of his health, but what?

There were no recorded visits after August 18, 1954. He had died

August 20, and this date was marked beneath the last visit. And "Deceased." No number followed.

I set the pile of photographs aside. I was hit with a sense of unease. I wasn't sure if I had a pile of nothing, or just didn't know enough to find out what I did have. I didn't know what to do, and I didn't feel much like thinking about it. It had been a trying night, after a trying day. I felt I could only function at a perfunctory level.

I lay down on the bed. The way I felt reminded me of the days following the teething nights of my daugher's first teeth. Hard times.

In a rush I remembered Eddie, the night watchman, and my stool, the fallen prisoner. It really made me feel bad. How can someone with my skills be such a poor breaker and enterer?

No nerves, that's how. Actually maybe just lack of practice. Idly I resolved to practice more. Maybe a life of crime. Idly I fell asleep.

12

A siren howled, but not for me. About a quarter after three. No day left hardly. My mind wasn't much refreshed either. Just enough that from the office I got a manila envelope, a looseleaf ring binder, a hole punch and a pair of scissors.

The envelope I filled with the pictures I had perused so fruitlessly in the morning. From their various drying locations I gathered the duplicate set that I had made in my early morning zeal. I congratulated myself on my zeal. I flattened the copies and punched holes in them to fit the binder. Then I cut the names and addresses off the records, and grouped them by person in the binder. I numbered each person's records.

If I couldn't read them, maybe a doctor could. Fishman was not the only doctor in town. I had a doctor of my own. How simple life is! Take the records to Dr. Harry and let him read them. All it would take was money. And a prayer, so to speak, that there was something on them to read.

I called Harry, but spoke to him only through his nurse. "What's he doing? Making dogfood out of one of his patients?"

"No, Mr. Samson," said the nurse. I've talked to her before. She took

59

my message to her boss and brought me one back in return. I would drop off the binder at his home. He would read them for me tonight.

I wrote a note to attach to the binder. I asked him to go over the records and look for "anything unusual," whatever that meant. These were the records of a general practitioner and his son for a family of patients.

Before I left, I wrote an equivalent mental note for myself. What I want you to do is . . .

Is what? It had been about twenty-four hours since I had thought explicitly about what I was trying to do—find the father of Eloise Graham Crystal, born November 1, 1954, in the city of New York.

What things could I do that hadn't yet been done? How about going to New York? I had lived in New York for a number of years. My child had been born there. Very interesting, but what could I find out in New York? Maybe Eloise's real father had visited Fleur in the hospital. Would there be records? Would a nurse there remember him?

No.

I could go to Europe and try to locate the conception spot. Where in Europe? Probably near the grave of Joshua Graham. How near? Ten miles? One hundred miles? Oh, yes, very useful. I could find out more exactly where and when they had been in various places in Europe. How? Ask Fleur? Not if she had the secret we presumed she did. Ask Leander? But how do you go up to a stranger and ask him for the itinerary of a sentimental trip he made seventeen years ago. "I'm writing an article. . . ." If he were gracious he would laugh.

Or maybe they had sent picture postcards. Mail. Mail to Daddy. Distinctly possible.

Distinctly on cue, Eloise Graham Crystal, client and juvenile, teeny benefactress, entered the office. She seemed to be becoming the punctuation for my workday.

She saw me in the back room as I saw her come in. She made straight for my personal quarters.

"So this is where you live," she said, not quite admiringly. She sat in what I consider my dining-room chair—it has wide wooden arms on which I balance plates and glasses. "So much junk," she said.

Fresh from sleep and idea, I chose not to defend the artifacts of my life. Instead I got to work. "I've thought of something you may be able to do," I said.

60

"What?" Her eyes were still wading through the room. I waited impatiently till she found me again. Just another piece of junk.

"Do you know where your grandfather's records are? Not his business records, but things like personal letters?"

"Yes, I think so. They're in some shoe boxes in the attic."

"Are you sure?"

"Mummy used to take me up there and show me them. I told you. All kinds, like from her brothers and from her. And old ones from people she says were important. I think he kept every letter that he ever got."

"I need to see them."

"All of them? There are boxes and boxes."

"I guess as many as I can, but mostly from your grandfather's later years and from the war years. Like the 1940's from your uncles and from 1952 and 1953 from anyone. Do you think you can get them?"

"*Me* get them?" It was just sinking in.

"You're the only person I know with easy access to the house."

"Couldn't I, like, just let you in and you get them?"

"Are you afraid?"

"I don't know. If I get caught, I guess so."

"Aren't you in a lot better position to explain it if you get caught than I am?"

"But it seems . . . Oh, well. When do you want them?"

"When can you get them?"

"Tonight I guess. But I can't take them out in the morning. You'll have to meet me tonight. I'll get them out and you can meet me."

"What time?"

"I guess about eleven thirty. I'll go out to the back and between houses. I'll meet you at the corner of Jefferson and Seventieth." She took a breath and giggled. "You'll recognize me OK. I'll be the one carrying boxes."

"Of course."

She stood up crisply and came to stand in front of me. She had just come to check in and now she had gotten lumbered with duties.

"Are you making progress?"

"I think so. But those letters will help."

"Will you find my biological father?"

"If he can be found I'll find him, or tell you how." Rashly.

"Good," she said. "I'm tired now. I have to go. Actually, I don't have to go, but I want to go. I came to town to do some shopping. See you tonight. Don't be late."

I had been looking up at her and feeling uncomfortable. She bounced away, and out of the office door. I frowned and wondered if I was incorrect in believing her skirts were getting shorter. Growing shorter before my very eyes.

I looked through the door after her for several seconds. I was having a peculiar reaction. Unease at the notion of a client breezing in and out at her will—to check up on me.

She was a client, fine. She had paid me, in advance, with the sizable sum of eleven hundred dollars. Her problem was a legitimate one, concerning as it did her own legitimacy. All well and good.

But on the other hand Eloise Crystal was just a kid and nobody, especially a free-lance personality, likes to be responsible to a kid.

But I knew she was a kid when I started.

Did I? Or did I see the young adult she had wanted to appear? Or did I see a job that was out of the ordinary? Or did I see a job, period, as opposed to none?

I was remembering that I had assumed, presumed, a very great deal. Basically because I wanted to, and possibly for reasons I didn't want to tell myself about.

If we were coming down to it maybe I was seeing more in my client than business. Me getting hooked on a kid? That would be a twist. But who knows how flexible one is?

I got up and stretched. I rubbed my face. I went to the sink and splashed some cold water on my face. I did all the things I do when I am on a tack I don't like.

It helped a little. When in trouble, go back to basics. Good basketball sense. I tried to figure out what it was that I wanted me to be doing.

Finding a father, right?

Because a kid did some blood tests, right?

I was embarrassing myself. What a hideous confused undirected mass I had become. I had broken into Fishman's office to get confirmation of the blood tests, and I hadn't even tried to find the blood types.

And I knew I wasn't going to either. It was a measure of my state of mind. I went to my pantry and took out a half-full bottle of mediocre bourbon. I also keep a bottle in my desk drawer for form's sake, but I usually get bluesy in my living quarters. I took a long belt. Scratch the day.

I went to the note I had written to Harry. At the bottom I added, "And find me the blood type for each of these too, if they're there."

Then I went back and had another crack at Poppa's baby bottle.

Isn't a detective allowed to get depressed?

Especially a detective who lives alone?

I realized that it was after dark and I had not been out of doors all day. That has an effect on a fellow.

I gathered my coat and burden of medical records and departed.

I drove very slowly. But it still didn't take very long to get there. Spann and Spruce. It's not really very far from where I hang my boots at night. Usually I like my world condensed. But not that night. Why couldn't I have a nice doctor living far enough away that a fellow could sober up before he got there? By driving slowly. Why didn't I have Fishman for a doctor? He was good and far away.

I was still upset about my episode at Fishman's.

Ah, well, we all have things we cringe at when we recall them. You just try to avoid thinking about them.

I was studiously not thinking about them when I arrived at Dr. Harry's.

"Phew! You smell like a still." It was Evvie, Harry's wife. She has a sweet tongue.

"These are for Harry," I said proffering my ring binder of medical records. Worthless fruit of a fool's sally. "I called him about them. There's a note." I smiled to be friendly.

She pinched them between her thumb and index finger and held them so they didn't touch her body.

"Are you catching?" she said.

It may be hard to believe but we are all good friends.

"I'll give them to him," she said. I just stood there grinning like the fool I felt. "So go away!" she said. "Shoo! He'll call you."

I showed her. I left.

I got in the car, rolled down my window and drove off. Slowly.

I had a decision to make. Having dropped off my package, getting into the air, on the road, had cleared my decks somewhat. But I still needed some activity for the evening that would let me out easily to pick up the letters at eleven thirty.

I considered calling Eloise and telling her to forget the eleven thirty business. To bring them in the afternoon.

I decided not to. Because I figured that I would want to look at them before the afternoon and because, somewhat more refreshed and charitable as I was, it occurred to me that she might have difficulties getting out except in the quieter parts of the night.

So. The Pacers or my woman. I called my woman.

Sweet thing that she is, she told me not to bother if I was going to leave before eleven thirty. And she's right. We have a working understanding about business; it doesn't fit. Hers or mine.

Pacers it was.

Until I arrived at the Fairgrounds Coliseum and deduced from a ticket stub in the street that the Pacers had played their second game of the season Friday night. This was Saturday: no game. The locked doors and darkened lights helped confirm my conclusion.

It broke my heart.

I went to see dirty movies at the Fox instead. What else can a fellow do to pass a lonely Saturday night?

13

After heady concentration on the other world of sex, what does a fellow need but a late-night tryst with a fair damsel, Maid Eloise?

I waited as instructed on the corner of Jefferson and Seventieth and at twelve I was beginning to wonder when I should get upset. No sooner wondered than I was presented with a vision turning my way from the alley corner. Even fancy houses in Indianapolis seem to have alleys. Eloise Crystal, nightgowned and bearing boxes, came bouncing toward me barefoot. Who is to say that movies are the unreal world?

I had one powerful headache.

I opened the door and she slid in beside me. Not just onto the seat, but beside me.

"It took me a long time," she said breathlessly. "To find the right ones and to get out of the house. I ran all the way. But I made it, didn't

I?" She looked up at me, her face reflecting streetlight madly. I wondered if she was high. I wondered if I was high.

What do you say? "You got them though," I said.

"I'm sorry I was coy with you in your office today. I don't want that to be the way I'm going to be." She took my hand and kissed it, and in almost the same moment she slid back out the door and broke through the street-lit patch of curb into the darkness of the alley mouth. A romantic vision for a simple man. Perhaps Maid Eloise would be more aptly appellated Just Plain Eloise.

What do you do with clients who kiss your bloody hand?

14

By the time I got home I was in no shape to sleep. I set myself to the letters, just a few before bedtime. She had brought seven boxes. Together they held an enormous quantity of paper. Into the wee hours I sorted letters by date, over fourteen hundred, in their original envelopes.

The oldest was from February, in some unclear year in the late 1800's; the last, from 1954 on the occasion of the death of Estes Graham.

They were not business letters, but many dealt with the business times of a life: marriage (1916, the first large pile); births of children (1920 Windom; 1922 Sellman, 1926 Joshua, 1930 Fleur); and a hundred or so on Irene Olian's death in 1937.

It was three in the morning. I didn't want to tackle them right away. I looked only at a few from the fringe. J.C. Penney had written to express sorrow for Irene.

Finally I slept.

Morning and a new sun. Old letters and bad coffee, not an enticing notion so I did the unusual and squeezed the juice and pulp out of six tiny oranges and had fresh same, for a change. After all, letters were a change, not my daily fare.

And in fact they did contribute new information. No hearty confessions, but some information. Like, the Leander-Fleur vacation of

1953-54 was spent primarily in and near Toulon, in France. There was one trip to Württemberg, Germany, one to Tours, France, and a trip to London. But letters to Estes arrived weekly, full of clipped good cheer, extolling the weather and the food with monotonous regularity.

These epistles surprised me somewhat. They were the first break in my image of Fleur. Not that I had known enough to say that she couldn't be airy. But I didn't expect consistency of mood over a period of months.

Between 1944 and 1945 were the rather different letters from Fleur's youngest brother, Joshua. Clear, but poorly scripted, full of complex thoughts squeezed into simple sentences.

August, 1944

My own dear Father and Sister,

I am not allowed to talk about where we are. I don't really want to think about that part of things.

I think all the time about you both, about Mrs. F. and about Win and Slugger. Hope they got better groups to live with wherever they are than I got. Purely a bunch of foul mouths here. . . .

I am curious about a man in war who can care about such things. His brothers were already dead when he wrote.

In December he made his first mention in letters home of a man ". . new transferred to my company. He is decorated for his bravery. I don't know why they sent him here. There is no call for bravery here. He is called Leander Crystal. He has been a friend to me. He don't use the bad mouthing of lots of the others here."

Joshua wrote of his friend in seven letters home—until he could write no more. Leander wrote of Joshua once.

March, 1945

Dear Mr. and Miss Graham,

I know by now you must have been informed officially of the tragedy which befell your fine young man, my friend Joshua. We are heartbroken here, as you must be there, because he was as

66

good a man as they come and would have made a fine fighting man had they given him the front-line experience he so badly wanted.

That you should know exactly the circumstances, Joshua was driving a truck filled with badly needed supplies when a French family appeared on the road before him. Pulling to the roadside to avoid them he triggered a mine on the road's shoulder and was killed. Although the roads are meant to be examined, these things are known to happen.

As it happens, I was nearby and rushed to poor Joshua with a doctor who I was walking with.

You should know that his last words were of his love for his father, his sister and his brothers. I cried as he died in my arms and I am not a crying man since I have endured without tears the deaths of others I had known much longer than your son.

It is such a tragedy that wars, even just ones, must be fought and that men such as your son must be lost. The extra tragedy is that men are lost other than to enemy bullets.

I felt I must write; I felt so close to your boy and I feel that already I almost know you. If I survive this war I may hope one day to visit you, for educational plans may bring me to your city.

Yours sincerely in this
time of sorrow,

Leander Crystal

It was information day on the ranch. It was just noon when Dr. Harry called.

"Lovely pile of shit you've saddled me with," he offered. "Well, you can't expect me to do much more on this than I've done. I don't know what the hell you're up to, but I hope you know what you're doing, obviously snooping around. I know if you ever did this for any of my patients I'd have you vasectomized."

"How's Evvie?"

"And I'll tell you this too, these records you've snatched are among the most meticulous and clearly written medical records I've ever seen.

Well organized. Only a dunce couldn't find for himself the things you wanted to know." There was a pause. "Evvie is fine. How've you been? She says you were a little frayed last night."

Harry is an acquired taste. He has violent, sarcastic turns of mood, but a gentle heart and soul. He is also flat-footed and has to wear special shoes. I've got a theory which connects them with his mouth.

With little more ado he provided the following information which he had culled from the records I had given him.

Number 1. Died from pneumonia in 1937. Blood type A. (Irene Olian Graham)

Number 2. Heart attack in 1945, strokes in 1952 and 1954. Died of heart seizure 1955. Blood type O. For some reason there is no note of the death certificate. Either an oversight or this doctor was not the certifying physician at time of death. Records are kept at a Health Department office, if this is important (Estes Graham)

Numbers 3, 4, and 5 in order of birth. Nothing of note. Blood types A, A, and O. (The brothers)

Number 6. Wide variety of complaints over the years, but very little really wrong. Presumably a hypochondriac (seemed to begin within a year after Number 1 died). She ran through all the symptoms of "popular" diseases: that is, the ones which were well publicized at the time, e.g., TB, pneumonia, heart. No doubt if alive now is worrying about cancer. Last recorded appointment for possible sterility, though the tests were never done and she appears to have stopped going to this doctor in August, 1953. That in itself is unusual unless she moved, because the doctor was clearly congenial. Blood type O. (Fleur Olian Graham)

Number 7. Little information, no significant appointments, colds, checkups and such. Stopped going to this doctor when Number 6 stopped. Blood type B. (Leander Crystal)

Number 8. This is complete and current record from two and a half weeks of age. Starting November 17, 1954, till about four weeks ago. Nothing unusual. Blood type A. (Eloise Graham Crystal)

"Well, there it is, you got it?" I had, in scribble form. "I don't know what a dolt like you is going to make of this stuff. So let it drop. You tell me something."

"Shoot."

68

"What are the relationships of these mysterious numbered corpses."

"In order. Mother, father, three sons, daughter, husband of the daughter, child of the daughter and her husband."

"Adopted child?"

"No."

"So at least I see why you asked about the blood types."

"You tell me."

"I'd explain it, but you are too dumb. Obviously because number six and number seven cannot be the parents of number eight. But for Christ's sake, Al, it's a little late for them to be disputing parentage, isn't it?"

"I guess it is."

He said quietly, "You know there is a lot of money represented here."

"How can you tell?"

Less quietly, "Because of all the appointments. We aren't in this business for nothing, you know. Speaking of not being in the business for nothing . . ."

We agreed on a stipend, somewhat less than the thousand dollars he suggested.

We also agreed that I would call on them sober when this was over and tell them about it all.

So there it was. Blood tests confirmed. Purported parentage disproved. A rich gift, in the circumstances. Enough to elate me in itself. I had a real case, a real client, and a real job.

My mind moved back to the letters. They had given me information on the non-father, Leander Crystal. Both the answer to why the Ames, Iowa, soldier had appeared in Indianapolis, and at the same time no answer. "Educational plans." Was the man in a war making educational plans detailed enough to know what new city he was coming to? Why Indianapolis? The weather? To play basketball? Or perhaps relatives of whom I as yet knew nothing.

Why is it that once you've found out something you really wanted to know, it's no longer so interesting?

He who elates easily also takes rapid falls. What the hell did I know anyway? Nothing, I had not one good lead to the real father.

Well, there was one, of course. Fleur Crystal. She should know if anyone did. Perhaps it was the time for bold action, frontal attack. Go see Fleur.

"OK, lady, no fucking around. Let's have it. This ain't a finger in my pocket, you know, and it's getting ready to blow. So spill, sister. It happened a long time ago, it ain't gonna hurtcha, so I want the true story now, sister, and fast." And when I got it, I'd hang on to it for a while to get some extra loot out of Eloise. No sympathy for nobody.

I dwelt on these aggressive notions for some time, long enough for one's room to appear definitely too small to hold one. The world was too small. I took an afternoon nap. Nice habit, if your work can accommodate it.

I awoke by unnatural means. Shaken into consciousness by an Eloise Crystal. Not a proper way to wake. Not a proper manner to leave lands of guitar music and naked ladies.

"Do you always sleep in your chair in the middle of the afternoon? You must be older than I thought."

Children can be cruel. "Do you always come around here in the afternoon? Nothing better to do? No Sunday schools out where you live?" Or haystacks? It was a balmy autumn Sunday.

For some reason she thought about it. "I guess I'm just hoping I'll be able to help. I've never been so close to the answer before, and I've never done anything so active about it, if you know what I mean." So close. Not exactly my phrasing. But she continued. "And besides, I find it sort of exciting."

No quarter! "You must lead a rich fantasy life." So close!

"I do," she said.

So I was awake. I stood up and went to the kitchen sink to rinse my face off. I returned to my client, who had dropped into the armchair I had been warming for her.

One thing for sure. The daylight Eloise was back. No giggles, no nighties, no gay rendezvouses. Perhaps finding me asleep really had done something to her. Shock and uncertainty. Ah, kids. Appearance is everything. I pulled up my dining-room chair and tried to ease her back into my world.

"The letters were useful. And I have also confirmed the blood typings you made."

70

Sharp look. "At last?"

"Look, Eloise, I do not need to sit around here trading stares and strategems with you. If you have nothing to add, then I do."

"What are you going to do?"

"The next major step is to go and see your mother."

A right answer for a change; glowing light. And I realized at once why. To go and see her mother, so to speak, was exactly what she had always wanted to do.

"You're not going to ask her right out, are you?"

"It depends. Probably not, not this time, but it will depend on how we get along."

"You'd better not go while Leander is there."

"Will he be there tonight?" Her face lit on tonight.

"One never knows."

"I'll give it a try."

"Don't call on the phone. She hates the phone."

"I won't." New communication. "And please don't be there while I'm there."

"Why not?"

"You might distract me."

"Me distract you?" She blushed.

"Yes."

She thought for a moment. "You must lead a rich fantasy life."

"It's not for children to throw words back in the faces of their elders." I was an elder, I could tell. I didn't blush.

"I'm not a child."

I laughed at her. Not loud, but clearly. And after a few moments she laughed too.

I made us tea. We chatted, which is what one is supposed to do over tea. She told me a little periphery about her school life, and that she didn't plan to go to college. All very nice. All very indirect. We didn't talk about our project at all.

15

Black-and-white pictures lie. I'm not sure what I had been expecting of Fleur Crystal, but whatever it was I was surprised. She had flame-red hair. Nobody had even hinted at it. My fault perhaps, not having asked for physical characteristics, yet somehow I felt it was so striking that people had cheated on me a little bit by not volunteering mention of it.

Shoulder-length, like Eloise. Fire head.

She had opened the door herself when I rang. Made up, jade earrings virtually scraping her bare shoulders. Madras halter top, a summer garment, and a full square-dance skirt. You've seen them, black with red and yellow figures sewn around above their hems. The sequence of figures might be telling a story but because of the folds you can never see enough of them to read what it is saying.

I was about to embark on the newspaper-story story when she invited me in. The house was very hot, winter heating on an autumn night. And it was full of cut flowers.

I followed as she swept into the living room, waved to a furry couch set between two flower-laden tables, and sat down there with me. We were close enough for me to smell liquor on her breath, but not close enough to touch.

I explained who I was. About my story on her father. Her eyes lit at mention of Estes Graham.

"How wonderful! You want to talk to me about Daddy. I can talk about Daddy."

"Are there people you can't talk about?"

"But of course. Isn't it meant to be the same for everyone?" She smiled, no, radiated at me, but somehow distantly. I felt her warmth, but it was not sensual. More a warmth of purpose. It felt austere. I felt very strange to be wanting to ask her if she had ever screwed away from home.

We went through most of the ordinary, by now, material about her father and mother and her brothers. Devotion oozed from her pores; sweat from mine.

"And then I married Leander. He's a good man, a wonderful man. I think if he left me I'd die."

"Is there any reason to think he's going to leave you?" Some people would have tossed me out on a question like that. She answered it, with the sort of smile that made her face seem grave. "Well, one never knows in this life, does one?"

"That's true. I understand you had a miscarriage recently. I'm sorry."

The face remained grave. "It wasn't so bad, except for my husband. He wanted more children so badly. So badly. But there is a high risk of miscarriage when a woman is over thirty." Say forty.

She continued. "It was twins." A brave smile. "These days"—and she paused—"but I've suffered through a lot of illnesses. And ill spirits too. I've really been quite hypo . . . thingy—"

"—chondriacal?" I offered.

"Right. Absolutely right. A cigar for the gentleman. Give the gentleman a cigar. How did you know about that?" It was not a question asked with the hardness of a woman tight with her information. I could have told her that she had just told me. Instead I said, "I spoke with a woman who used to work for your father. A Mrs. Forebush."

An abrupt change of mood. From manic camaraderie to squinty-eyed attention. "Just what all did she tell you?" I was not prepared for the change. I had not had time to adjust to the nuances.

"Not really anything more than you have told me now."

The squint remained. "And did she tell you that she did everything she could to get my father to marry her? Did she tell you that, Mr. Newspaper Man?"

"No, she didn't."

"And did she tell you that she never was married and that she just picked up the 'Mrs.' because she had a daughter. And the daughter died, which was only just. Did she tell you that?"

"No."

"Well." The word was a final one. She sat back, but words filled in the space. "One thing about Daddy, he could always tell about people. Mrs. Forebush so called just did not measure up. Do you know that at the time Daddy died she even had the nerve to suggest—"

But I didn't get a chance then to find out what Mrs. Forebush had the nerve to suggest, or to get a chance to decide whether to screw up my courage and ask the answer to the real question I was interested in.

In the doorway stood a dapper bald gentleman, about 5 feet 7, in a

suit of contemporary cut which fitted him quite as well as his Army
uniform had. The pictures had done him justice, even offered mercy.
Not a handsome man, but a man with bearing and presence.

In the middle of her sentence Fleur wilted. She bolted from the couch
and walked in front of me to a door in the wall at my right. She
disappeared through it. When she closed it behind her I finally turned
my attention back to the other side of the room. It was he, Leander
Crystal, then.

"Who are you?" Tense, demanding response, but without the hostility
in the voice which shone in his eyes. In action the man was performing
a necessary task, solving a problem. As he spoke layers of wrinkles
made and unmade themselves on his forehead. He was fascinating to
watch. His voice required more than watching, however. I told him
about the newspaper article.

"Please give me the name of someone at the paper with whom I can
check what you say."

I gave him Maude's name and title, and would have given him her
number, but he stopped me because he wanted to get the number from
the phone book. Suspicious chap. I would have given him the public
line, not her private phone. I wouldn't have cheated him.

When he left the living room bound for the room that contained the
phone I thought for a moment I was alone. But I was wrong. Fleur
Crystal's head was in the room with me. She was peeping back from
whatever room she had gone to. How she knew Leander had gone I did
not know, but she knew.

I was decidedly uncomfortable and she cowered in the doorway.

"You shouldn't be here."

"Oh, come on, Mrs. Crystal. Surely there is nothing in our talking that
could be offensive to your husband."

She was not reassured. In fact she said again, "You shouldn't be here."

I sighed and sat down again. The emotional weather had been
changing so much that my surface sensibilities were beginning to erode.
It was leaving only the rock inside. I took another deep breath,
regretted that I didn't smoke, so I didn't have a cigar to light up to foul
the room. I remembered, Fleur had talked of cigars. I'd have bet that
her father smoked them.

Leander returned to light me up.

"You seem authentic enough, Mr. Samson, but I'm going to have to ask you to leave now anyway. You certainly should not have approached members of my family without consulting me first."

"Your wife owns to being over twenty-one, Mr. Crystal, meaning no offense. And if I am trying to find out about Estes Graham, do I go to his child, or to his child's husband?"

"In point of fact, you go to neither. You will get no more help here. You will leave now. And, to be frank, it's not much of a story, at this late date. Time to go home. This way please."

I went. But I didn't like it.

And I didn't go home. I went on a drive around the north side. I had plenty to keep me occupied. Heavy thinking. Like how unusual Fleur Crystal was. A complex, mad woman with a lot more I wanted to know, whether she would ever tell me or not. In the end what bugged me most was Fleur's utter change when Leander came in. Self-sufficiency, of a sort, which had become complete subservience. It was spooky.

At night, alone, I spook easy. I found a phone booth and I called milady. We set the date for an hour because I needed time to get the whole business a little further out of my system. So I wouldn't be thinking of it there.

I took the long drive to the south side slowly. I turned on the radio. I stopped for some fancy ice cream. Usually I bring something because it makes her happy and that makes me happy. Earlier I had been thinking of flowers, but when it came right down to it, I had seen my fill of flowers for the night.

I woke up for a few moments in the middle of the night. I don't remember the dream. But I woke up knowing that I had to see Mrs. Forebush. I tossed and turned for a while about whether it would be better to wait for afternoon or to go in the morning. Finally I did get back to sleep.

16

A dark rainy day. A Monday harbinger of winter. Another winter, a thirty-seventh winter. Not good weather for the soul.

About eleven o'clock I was at Mrs. Forebush's door. Coffee hour. My former father-in-law once explained that eleven is a proper time to visit someone with whom you don't want to stay a long time. To fulfill social obligations.

The yellow flower was gone from Mrs. Forebush's hair. So too much of the smile which I had hoped for, even expected.

When she opened the door to me she said, "This morning I had a call from Leander Crystal. For various reasons he has asked me not to speak with you again. I don't know what you've been up to, Mr. Albert Samson, but this is most unlike Mr. Leander Crystal."

"I'm sorry if I have been causing trouble for you, Mrs. Forebush. It was not my intention."

"I'm glad you feel that way. I've decided that I shall speak to you anyway, as long as you will answer some questions for me as well. Come in, Mr. Albert Samson."

As we sat down she said, "First, young man, you must tell me what it is that you are really doing. On reflection I find your article story hard to buy. You didn't ask me the appropriate questions."

"I'm a licensed private detective."

"I thought as much. Who employs you, Fleur or Leander?"

"I don't think that it is what you think it is, Mrs. Forebush. I've been hired by Eloise."

"Little Eloise! Whatever for?"

Nitty gritty time. "Before I can talk about that I'll need some assurance from you—"

She cut me off. "Oh, piffle. We had an understanding when you left here three days ago. You know we did; that's why you felt at ease coming back here to talk to me. As long as you are working in the best interests of the child, we are working together, and you have no need to worry about anything that I might tell or not tell anybody."

She was right, of course. We had an understanding.

"Eloise came to me convinced that Leander Crystal was not her real father. She hired me to find her real father."

The old lady grew older, dropped to the back of the chair from her perch on the front edge, and considered this information. From the back of the chair she asked, "And have you found the man?"

"I have confirmed Eloise's supposition."

"Beyond doubt?"

"Beyond doubt."

"And again, Mr. Albert Samson, have you found the man?"

"No. I have found that Eloise was conceived while Fleur was in Europe with her husband."

"Oh, my."

"As well, I've been to see Fleur, last night. But Leander ushered me out."

"I see."

"From what you say, he must have pumped Fleur to find out what she told me. I mentioned to her that I had talked to you."

"And coming here today, what did you think that you wanted from me?"

"When Leander came in last night Fleur was telling me that when her father died you had made some suggestion that she did not approve of. I wanted to know what that was."

She did not seem happy. "Poor Estes," she said. "I don't see how that can reflect on the object of your investigation."

"If you don't want to tell me, Mrs. Forebush, I have no way to make you." Except the one I was using. It was she who had first verbalized our "understanding."

"All right. All right. It is not much of a story, but at the time I was not entirely satisfied with the circumstances of Estes' death. It seemed to me . . . Well, it was Mr. Crystal who found him after the heart attack. Estes was on the floor beside the bed reaching for the buzzer to my room. They said he must have felt pain and fallen out of bed reaching for the buzzer. Now I had pinned that buzzer to his sheet before I went to sleep."

"I see."

"On the other hand there is no question that he died of a heart attack, and I suppose he could have pulled the buzzer off the sheet and dropped it on the floor as he fell. It could have been that way. I was upset. It just wasn't a very happy time." Nor for Fleur, who might well remember such an accusation out of the proportion dictated by the actual circumstances.

"I'm very sorry to have brought all this up, Mrs. Forebush. But I wanted to know. I'm sorry to have put you through it."

She thought about that for a while. "I'll survive," she said. "One of the problems with being older is that there are more things you don't like to talk about."

"One more thing and I'll leave. This one is more to the point. If Leander Crystal suspected that Fleur's child was not his own, would he just sit by and let her have it, and then raise it as his own?"

More thought. Her eyes wandered about the violet room, in contrast to the lack of motion in her stiff, drawn lips. Had she remained silent a little longer I would have gone off myself, thinking about age and death and failure. The violet of the room had drawn in closer and become a little darker. What a bad day. And what a poor way to start it.

Finally she said, "I wouldn't have thought so. But who can tell. I'm hardly an expert on Mr. Crystal."

"Well, could Fleur have been raped and not told Leander about it?"

She thought again. "I just can't see the Fleur of those days keeping anything back—either from her father or Mr. Crystal."

We sat and thought about that. There was not a great deal more to be said.

I took my leave.

17

It was still raining. The wet stuff made me move to my car faster than I wanted to. I got in, and drove away from the front of the house. I took a right at Central and drove for a while heading vaguely for the center of town. I stopped at a nondescript luncheonette. When you have time for lunch, it's lunchtime. I had tea and a piece of squishy chocolate cake.

Through the window next to my table I watched some construction men watching the rain from inside the shell of an extension to a public school. Why they were just standing inside and watching the rain I finally figured out. They had built the frames for concrete steps up to the new wing's door, but they didn't want to pour the cement while the rain was heavy.

I had a wave of strong feeling that I didn't want them to pour the steps ever. I appreciated the rain for stopping them. The headlines would read "Samson's Rain Prevents Cement."

Tires cutting through water on the street make just about the same sound as a fork cutting through squishy chocolate cake. Minds wander.

I had some time. My notebook bore two instructions that I decided to get done: "Check will"; "check death certificate."

I decided to be bold and do the hard one first; the death certificate.

Records of deaths in Indianapolis are kept at the Board of Health on West Michigan Street. The certificates are hard to see because only a little of the information they record is treated as a public record. To be precise, "name and sex, age, place of death, and residence of the deceased." That is specified in Section 1227 Chapter 157, of the Acts of 1949 of the State of Indiana. I know. I have had run-ins with Miss Moleman before. Miss Moleman, guardian of the death certificates of Marion County.

"Estes Graham. Male. Eighty-three. Graham House, North Meridian Street. Same," said Miss Moleman. I call her Moose. Not because of any physical similarities—it's just the things she says to me are as sweet as a hunter's moosecall.

"Come on, honey," I said. "It's not going to hurt to let me have a look at that little old green piece of paper."

"No," she said.

"I'll take you out for a piece of chocolate cake."

"My instructions are to provide the information I have given you and nothing more. To see the original death record you have to have a court order. Do you have a court order?"

I sighed. I had tried.

Miss Moleman is a locked door. The key to Miss Moleman is Miss Fitch, her supervisor. The key to Miss Fitch is Maude Simmons. The key to Maude Simmons is money. One prefers to save a client's bread, but it can't be done with Miss Moleman. One of many things that can't be done.

79

I took a left in the corridor outside Miss Moleman's domain. I headed for the nearest available public phone. It was downstairs next to a window in the Health Department lobby. I could see the parking meter I'd parked my car at. I'd thought I was going to be lucky this time. Here it was raining and I'd found a meter with half an hour on it right in front of the office. But, no. Miss Moleman was not at home in bed with the flu. And I was on the phone to the Indianapolis *Star*.

I called Maude. Maude called Miss Fitch. Miss Fitch walked from her office into the record room, and withdrew a file. She had it in her office by the time I made my way up from the phone. I crossed her palm with five dollars—ten more later to Maude.

I had my wicked way.

You may never see a death certificate, crammed though it is with useful information. Estes Graham had died August 20, 1954. Coronary occlusion. No autopsy. He was a "businessman." He did not live on a farm. His mother's maiden name was Graham. The last attending physician was a Henry Chivian. He was buried by the Happy Hoosier Funeral Parlor on August 24, 1954.

OK. Duly noted.

I thanked Miss Fitch and handed her the file. She got up and returned it to Miss Moleman. As I left I walked by Miss Moleman's room. I thought I heard sobbing.

The rain had let up a little. I drove happily back downtown.

The City-County Building is a block from my house, but because of the rain I decided to try to get a parking place closer to it. I was lucky again. A metered spot within a stone's throw. I gave the machine a dime and threw myself across the street.

Probated wills are public records. But for no good reason it took me longer to get the one I was looking for than it had taken me to see the death certificate. But I persisted, and was rewarded.

It was a clean old document, dated December 12, 1937. It had stood as written since that date, a testament to Estes Graham's single-mindedness. The only changes were the deletion of the names of the three sons. A single inked line through each name. Initialed, dated, witnessed. When you finally got to names and disposition of funds, after several pages.

It was not what I would call your will in the street. It had been written following the death of Estes' wife, and it began with a long tribute describing her and their marriage.

Apparently the marriage had been accompanied by a complete change in Estes' life-style. Through his labored, God-fearing prose it was very clear that he loved the lady and attributed all the virtues and values of his life to her. His pre-Irene life was summed up as "worthless dissipations of life's energies." From what I could make out, reading fast, Estes' marriage to the lady had been something akin to a religious conversion.

Of the estate, a third had gone to something called the Billy Lee Olian Foundation. I checked my notes. Billy Lee was Irene's preacher father.

The remaining assets were to be held in trust for Estes' heirs. Half to his children. Half of the remaining half to their children. Half of that half to their children. And from what I could make out, so on till Judgment Day.

But there was a most peculiar catch. The heirs could draw the trust income as it occurred, but ". . . the capital of the trusts shall be available to an heir, in the proscribed proportion, only on first birthday of the first healthy child born in wedlock to the heir."

It continued to the effect that healthy children were a "God sign"; that they showed that a marriage was "approved of from above"; and that his own marriage had been proof of it.

Which could only mean that prior to his marriage in 1916 at the age of forty-five he hadn't fathered any healthy children who'd lived to be a year old.

In the same package as the will were the details of probate. The estate was worth a little under six million smackers, after inheritance taxes.

I went back over the operative clause. It meant that on the first of November, 1955—Eloise's first birthday—Fleur Graham Crystal had picked up a little less than two million dollars.

It meant that my client was in line for the same amount when she got married and started to breed.

It meant that the miscarried twins had saved my client a million dollars plus.

That's a lot of dollars. Eloise was right. She had money.

I finished my notes and checked my watch. It was pushing five, much later than I'd thought. Research has a way of eating up time.

On my car I discovered a parking ticket.

And a soaking wet parking ticket at that.

How can you take a soaking wet ticket into your car and put it in your notebook to deal with later? There's no way to handle a wet parking ticket reasonably.

Except to throw it away.

I whistled as I drove the block home.

Home held a note from Eloise. "I wish you'd been here today. They had a fight after you left last night. I'll come tomorrow." It was unsigned.

I didn't much like the note. Especially the implicit instruction, "be here tomorrow." No, I didn't fancy that. So I put aside the digestion of the details I had picked up during the day and concentrated on preparing to digest some food.

Food can clean the slate and provide a break for a fresh start on something. That evening it was trying to rehash some of the information that had managed to confuse me all day. I came up with two new conclusions.

The first was that I might be working both for my client and against her. If I found the information that would satisfy her psychologically—the information I had been hired to find—I might be cutting her out of her granddaddy's dough. This depended on legal things—whether the will was valid in its terms for requiring an "in-wedlock child," whether she was such a child, and whether the lapse of time might void any circumstances that would have been a problem before.

But I was being premature. I was presuming that there ever would be a time when the choice was available. So where was the father I was supposed to be finding?

Which led to the second point. Mrs. Forebush seemed to rule out all the possible ways for Fleur to become pregnant with Eloise.

Odds against a consenting affair were a million to one.

And if raped, odds very much that she'd have told Leander, who in turn would not be likely just to accept a rape-conceived child.

It didn't leave me much. I would be hard-pressed to believe that Fleur became pregnant without knowing it, that is to say, without being conscious of the act at the time or shortly afterward. Fleur is knocked unconscious or drugged somehow, somewhere (by accident or on

82

purpose) and is raped, gently. She then wakes up and her head hurts so much that she doesn't notice any other symptoms.

But these conceivabilities were strictly out of context. Specifically, the context of Leander. Where's hubby while this is going on? Off gadding? Knocked out by her side?

Altogether much too fantastic for me just to assume it by excluding other possibilities.

Which left me where I started: an affair or a conscious rape.

The affair—a million to one; odds established by Florence the Hoosier. I believed them myself, having met Fleur. Not unattractive, but motivated by nonsensual things. Looking for love, but not a kind sex had anything to do with.

So rape. Of course any lady can get raped, I suppose. The key here was not whether it could have happened, but the reaction of Leander.

So what did I know about Leander Crystal? Would he raise as his own a child he knew could be another man's?

The Ames, Iowa, said no. The Army hero said no. The "son-in-law" of Estes Graham tossing a booze-bearing reporter out of a party said no. Mrs. Forebush said no. The man who worked Fleur's share of the old man's money back to the ten-million-dollar bracket said "not unless there was a profit in it."

A profit. Like the million and a half to play with. It was true that Eloise had been worth a couple of million to the man.

The thought fascinated me. The bald man with a wrinkly forehead ushering me out of his house in the suavest of manners. The great protective father. Flesh peddler of his wife for the good old American profit motive.

Dates jumped from my notebook. Married 1949. First child 1954. Did that mean four years finding out they didn't hit it? Fleur's last, uncompleted appointment series with Fishman was a test for sterility. Maybe there was a similar intention to test Leander. And he, afraid of the results, had jumped from the family doctor, from Estes' doctor, to someone else, to a doctor with whom they could more easily keep the secret.

And then? After some unknown tests, off to Europe on the purported purpose of "visiting Joshie's grave." How long would that have taken? Nearly seven months?

And there? Leander arranges for someone to father his wife's child.

83

Not exactly middle-class Protestant ethic, but good solid profit motive.

And it required one simple presumption. That Leander and Fleur knew about the terms of Estes' will. The rest would follow. No rape at all. Fleur's utter devotion to her husband could be asexual enough for her to allow anything sexual.

I took a pause from the day's occupation. I was leaping ahead. Too far ahead and too fast.

My theory was untenable. The basic fact which supported it destroyed it. Fleur's recent miscarriage. Surely the presumption must be that Leander was the father of those twins. Yet that fact was not established either.

One thing was becoming abundantly clear to me. I didn't know much about Leander Crystal, and it was time to correct the situation.

Before bed I made preparations to do just that.

18

The alarm went off at 5:30. I guess that is because in my enthusiasm from the night's hypothesizing, I set it to go off at 5:30.

It was awful.

I struggled out of bed by a quarter of six, breakfasted to the extent of making a full pot of coffee and four pieces of toast. While the coffee brewed and the toast burned I went through the refrigerator pulling ice, milk, a very hard salami, and all my fruit, celery, and tomatoes.

While the butter was soaking through the night-sky toast, I rinsed my thermos jug and my cooler chest. While I was about it I got out some cookies and peanuts.

Then, as if one rested every seventh minute, I ate my toast and drank the three-fourths cup of coffee that did not fit in the thermos bottle.

Everything else into the cooler chest. Picnic time. By 6:15 I was ready to leave. Cunningly I had already packed a bag of nonperishables—two books, an unfinished crossword puzzle to write, from the *Morning Telegraph* the forms of the horses running at all the New York and California tracks, a book of paper and some crayons, a raincoat and sweater in case it got wet or cold, sunglasses in case it got sunny, mustache and floppy hat in case I got bored and wanted to laugh at myself in the car mirror. Camera and film, of course, for souvenir snapshots; a radio, a few miscellaneous tools and picks, my notebook and some money in case I forgot anything. It's a fairly large quantity of goodies to carry, but I packed it very tidily.

By 6:38 I was parked a discreet distance from the Crystal house.

I was waiting for Leander. A typical day. Or days. I wanted to find out things about him, right?

Tailing is one of the dullest of jobs. But I didn't have a whole lot else that I wanted to do. I didn't really know anything about Leander Crystal. I was hoping that at least I could find some people to talk to about him by going along after him for a day or two. Ultimately to get a better idea of how he operated—if he operated. Maybe it would only take a day—if I was a little lucky. And if I was very lucky maybe I would come across something more useful. Like a written confession.

At 6:40 I had a problem. What to do to amuse myself first. I settled for radio news and drawing pictures of animals of the jungle.

At 7:15 he came out, and drove off in his year-old Buick. I followed, drawings at my side, humming "Me and My Shadow."

For a tail I was in a pretty good mood. I draw a mean hippopotamus.

I spent three and a half hours observing the front of an office on Vermont Street. One of the plaques next to the door read "Graham Enterprises." I kept pretty chipper almost the whole time. The sun peeked tentatively out and then arrived to stay.

Merely learning about Graham Enterprises gave me a whole new game to play. Now I could always spend a day checking up on the people Leander must come in contact with daily here—garagemen, elevator men, secretaries, colleagues.

Around 11 I had a bad daydream. I saw myself picked up by a cop for loitering. Thrust before a judge to explain why I'd been sitting in my car on Vermont Street for three hours.

But that wasn't the bad part. The bad part was explaining to the judge why I was following Leander Crystal when what I wanted to know was who had knocked up his wife.

At 11:30 he came out. No briefcase. Of course he had had none when he went in. Back to the garage for the car. I was glad we were going for a ride.

Crystal drove with patience and courtesy. He headed north and for a while I thought he was going home for lunch. Not exactly typical of an Indianapolis executive, but millionaires have certain prerogatives.

But the north became northwest. And then became the Broadland Country Club. Not exactly a source of childhood memories for me. At a discreet distance I followed him into the parking lot. I pulled in as far away as I could get from his car. There is no guard or check station for members. But they do have a parking lot attendant. After a while he came over to give me a hard time. I explained that I was waiting for my sister-in-law who was having lunch after a swim. He bought it for a bit.

I would have ambled around the grounds for a while, never having compared an Indianapolis country club to those I'd been squired around in the East. But I wanted to minimize the risk that I would miss Crystal when he came out. At about 12:40 I drove back out to the main road.

After waiting till 1:20 at the edge of the pavement I was reasonably certain that more than lunch was being engaged in. That meant booze, bath, swim, golf, cards or broad. I sat where I was. It was the hardest part of the day. I found I had already read one of the books I had picked the night before.

He almost spotted me. The car was on the shoulder about 500 yards from the country club gate. A safe distance. But only about 10 yards from a tee. If I had realized that, I might have seen him come on it. As it happened I spotted him in the middle of his shot. Pure accident. But pure carelessness. One has to know where one is as well as where the subject is if one is to tail anybody with any professionalism.

Instead, I heard the swish of a practice stroke and looked left in time to see the man in action. His walk and his in-house bearing were nice but didn't do justice to his grace and flexibility. He was good and a pleasure to watch. In the second I had to watch him. As soon as I thought of it, I hit the seat of the car and waited too long—to be absolutely certain he had gone away.

In this kind of "sampling" tail—when you just want to see what the man does with his time—it is essential that he not know you are there. The fact of your presence will change what he does. It's the basic scientific problem. To observe phenomena without affecting those phenomena. And it's the problem which is the basic limit to observation.

There are other kinds of tail. Sometimes you go out of your way to make sure the guy knows you are tailing him. In divorce stuff, for example, sometimes you can't figure out on which stop he is making his extra woman so you can let him know you're following him and then see which place he avoids. If the guy is smart enough to realize you are following him.

On a tail you get a lot of time to generalize about being on a tail.

By 3:15 I was bored to tears. My ice had melted, my salami stank. I was listening to the same news and same records. I was not in the mood for speculation about what my subject was doing or who I might find who could get me into the country club on another day. I guess I'm just not very good on tails. I was suffering over the decision whether to continue it for another day. That's what really hurt. Not having a ready excuse to quit.

It's a good thing that there was little else in the area besides the country club, or I might have missed him coming out. I might have missed him anyway only he drove by me, headed back to town. He came out just in time. A few more minutes and I would have been making up some of the sleep I lost getting up so early in the morning.

We headed east and south, back toward town. I was guessing the office. That's what you get for guessing. I nearly cracked up switching lanes when he headed off to the right—south on Capital. Of course you've got to figure a guy can have someplace else to go in the world.

So we were heading south. And a degree of interest was creeping back into my stultified mind. I tried to suppress it. I hate being disappointed. Maybe he had a dentist appointment. Maybe he wanted the scenic route home so as not to surprise his wife in bed with the father of her child.

But the south side?

I mean, I like it because I grew up there, southeast anyway, but it's not everybody's notion of scenic.

We kept on going, down Capital, then a jog across McCarty to Madison. It looked like we were going out of town; Madison is Route 431 and it goes to Franklin, a fine town. In fact technically maybe we were out of town, on the right side of Madison, which is the city limits for a while.

But just in time, he turned off. Still in the city, near something called Southern Plaza.

For the first time all day I was having no boredom trouble. This must be some dentist he was going to. I was interested to see the color of her hair.

At Southern Plaza we took a left on Monkward Avenue and half a block down he pulled into the parking lot of a one-story office complex.

When I saw him go into the lot I speeded up and drove by its entrance. At the first cross street I made a U-turn as fast as my aging steed allowed and I fairly gunned it the half block back to Crystal's new office building. He got out of his car and walked toward the lobby door.

If I hadn't seen him get out of the car I wouldn't have known it was him. He was wearing sunglasses and he was walking underneath a newly acquired full head of hair which covered most of what I previously would have identified as his forehead.

I pulled up next to a parked car across the street to watch the spectacle. He entered the lobby and I saw him turn to his right as he left my line of sight. I waited a few minutes to see if he headed that way temporarily and then I found myself a parking place of my own. And I stepped across the street.

Inside the front door the lobby was lushly planted with plastic trees and bushes. It was utterly without chairs to hide in or pillars to hide behind. He had turned right into a single corridor which presumably ran the length of the wing. A similar corridor opened to the left.

I went back outside. I walked along the windows to the right of the front door, hoping to get a glimpse of him. I wanted to know which office he was in. Some notion of what he was doing in there.

I didn't see a thing, even though most of the offices had their blinds open. The building was five offices long. I was now reasonably certain that he had gone into one of the offices on the back side of the building.

I went around the end of the building. There was a storm fence four or five feet from the back sidewall. I turned the corner. Without walking down the row I could see that virtually all the blinds were shut—it was afternoon—facing southwest.

I went back to the front door, and went in.

The registry bore no names I was familiar with. Most of them were

88

businesses, presumably small. A teacher placement agency. Real-estate company. And some with unrevealing names. And by count seventeen names were listed. Which jibed with a notice which read, "Office space available. Reasonable rates. Full services," and gave a phone number which I took down. There was not much to be done. I was back at the waiting game.

Crystal was down the right wing somewhere. I headed down the left and picked an office at the end, "Import-Export Experts, Inc. Please Knock Before Entering."

out of. I figured I would be adequately inconspicuous if I was quickly

And I stood. The idea was to wait and see what office Crystal came ducking into another office.

He was inside for forty-eight minutes. Long enough for me to check that the locks used in the building were Braversweigs, and to realize none of the offices in the group did any overwhelming amount of people-to-people business. Phones rang, typewriters wrote, but nary a soul entered or left while I was standing there. I got lonely.

I did learn that inside my office I would find at least one female with a smooth cool voice. She was on the phone for the last twenty-seven minutes I was outside her door. The call was not exactly business. It had been some time since anybody talked on the phone like that to me. I was looking forward to going in.

At 4:33 Leander Crystal, shaded and bewigged, entered the corridor from the fourth office on the left in the far wing. As he locked his door by key, I broke in on Import-Export Experts, Inc. I didn't knock. It was not in the cards; my knuckles bruise easily.

I startled the chubby lady on the phone.

"What the fuck do you want?" Then she spoke more conciliatorily into the receiver cuddled twixt shoulder and ear.

"Some nut just came in without knocking—let me call you back." As she hung up and righted herself from a compromising position, she tactfully inquired, "What's the matter, mista, can't ya read? It says to knock before you come in here!"

I went to the door and opened it in. "Oh, yeah. So it does. Gee," I said, "I'm awfully sorry."

"What do you want?"

"I wanted to know what countries you import from."

"We can import from just about anywhere. What do you want imported?"

"Stamps," I said. "I'd like stamps from any foreign countries you can get them from. I thought that if you do business with foreign countries that you might get foreign stamps that I could have. I could pay you for them. Not much, but something."

She leaned back in her lean-back chair. "Jeesus." She rubbed her temples with her left hand. She sighed. "You don't look like no stamp collector."

"Well, I'm hoping to sell them. That's why I can pay a little."

"I'm sorry, mista. But the stamps we get here we save for the boss's kids. He'll be here tomorra morning if you want to come in then."

"Maybe I will. I'm sorry I bothered you." Then, as I was leaving I said, "You have a very nice voice," and closed the door.

I got to the lobby in time to watch Crystal pull out of the lot. I bolted across the street to my car door and saw him waiting at the light at the end of the block—Madison. The big question was whether he would be setting off back to the city, or whether he would take a new direction. The big decision was whether to keep after him, or settle for this secret recess of his life.

When the light went green, he turned right, the direction of central Indianapolis. Not that he might not have some other business I would want to find out about, but his staying in town made it all somehow more finite and contained if it did exist. Somehow more accessible on another day if I needed it.

And the idea of leaving a cozy place like Imports-Exports to go back on a tail, well . . .

I decided to stick around. I found a pay phone and made some calls. The first to my office.

It was 4:46, prime time. The phone rang twice before it was picked up. A tentative, female, familiar voice coughed and said, "Mr. Samson's office."

"Miss Crystal, this is Albert Samson."

Immediately more confident she said, "Gee, you've never called me Miss Crystal before."

"I hoped I'd catch you. I wanted to let you know I was on the job, and that I'd probably be in tomorrow. There are some things I want to ask you."

90

"Like about what?"

"Mostly about your environmental father and what he does with his day."

"He goes to the office in the morning and then to the country club for the afternoon."

"Every day?"

"Yes. Except weekends."

"Can you get in touch with him at the country club?"

"Only in an emergency. He doesn't like to be bothered. But if we have to, we call and ask for him."

"And when does he come home at night?"

"Sometimes early or sometimes he stays late. You can't tell."

"Well, we'll talk more about it tomorrow, if that's convenient."

"Oh, sure. I guess so."

"Maybe I should hire you as my secretary while we're about it."

She giggled. Not as charming a giggle as I'd heard through my Import-Export door. Too childish.

"Did you mind? I mean me answering the phone like that? I thought when it rang it might be something important."

"That's just fine, no problem. I'm glad you did."

"Yes, so am I."

And thus we parted.

For my edification I looked up the number of the Broadland Country Club.

"Is Leander Crystal there please?"

A formal male voice answered passionlessly and immediately, "Mr. Crystal is on the golf course."

"Is it possible to have him paged? It's a matter of life and death."

"If you'll leave your name and number, I'll have him call you back when he comes in."

"About how long will that be please?"

"Should be within an hour."

"Well," I said huffily, "it's not all that important." And I hung up.

Crystal was presumably returning to the club. More prerogatives of the rich.

Loath to leave a machine which had rewarded me so handsomely, I dialed the number on the notice posted in the Crystal Secret Office Building. I got through to Armor Realtors and learned that there were

91

two choice offices that happened to have fallen vacant last week. I inquired about the rent because one must, and made an appointment to see them the next morning.

Twenty offices and two vacancies; yet only seventeen were identified on the register in the lobby. I was willing to bet which office the odd one was.

19

On my way back to town I stopped at Bud's Dugout for food and to make sure Mom was keeping my bail money warm. I took my time and had a big meal. A last supper, one might say.

And I fed the pinball machine until the teacher couple came in. There is something that depresses me about people keeping regular schedules for their pleasures as well as their labors. But I may have been in a tenuous mood. It had been a long day, and the day was getting longer. A sunny, deceptively warm day.

After Bud's I stopped briefly at my office. The mail provided nothing which attracted my affections apart from a circular from something called Cosmic Detectives offering a course with Special Features. I dropped the bulk of my tailing gear and picked up my camera's close-up kit and keys and bag of tricks. I also divested myself of all identification.

By 8:00 p.m. I was back in South Indianapolis. I parked in the Southern Plaza shopping center, and bought a lot of film in the drugstore there. Then I took the walk to my moonlight adventure.

Outside the window of Crystal's office I felt a certain oppression from my own repetitiveness. I would have gone in the front—I have the keys to do it—but I didn't want to spend time standing in front of the door picking out the right key. The back was the better bet, and there was less chance of an alarm on individual windows than on the front door.

I was getting practice. It was good for me; I got in without my stool.

The room was not big, but he made plenty of use of it. Storage files, books, a big desk. Clothes. There was a washbasin with a fully stocked medicine cabinet—all the ablutionaries. He had his own private john. A single bed.

There was no trace of any woman.

The items of most interest looked to be the contents of the desk and files. I decided to photograph it all, and sort it out later.

There was plenty to take. Page by page through interminable financial records. Three drawers of the file. None of it meant anything to me offhand. I saw occasional names and dollar signs, but mine was not to reason why, for the moment. The bottom drawer was correspondence. I had shot seven rolls of film by the time I got to the desk.

In the desk drawers I got more goodies. Like a drawer of cash. A scrapbook in another and an address book and a pornography collection in the bottom.

For modesty's sake I started with the money. It was all twenty-dollar bills. I shot it so I could count the number of edges, and I took a few random serial numbers. Next drawer . . .

By ten thirty I had shot thirteen rolls of 36-exposure film. I had had to plug in my electronic flash.

I was about halfway through the pornography when a key slipped in the lock. I bolted upright. I'd been overconfident, uncautious. Being interrupted was the farthest thing from my mind. The door flew open and a voice of authority said, "Hold it right there, buster."

I was so surprised, startled, that I reacted with the intelligence of a small boy caught pinching Donald Duck at the comic rack. I guess I tend to panic under pressure. A failing. I ran for the door.

That was dumb, incredibly dumb. He was in the door I tried to run through.

More than that he had a gun on me.

Christ, he could have killed me!

I'm glad he was cooler than I was. Instead of shooting he clobbered me on the side of my head with the side of his gun.

I thought it had gone off. I have a vague recollection of some sort of strange feeling. I must have been falling.

They say I fell on my electronic flash. I must have hit it with my head. It broke.

20

I woke up with fuzz in my face. Fuzz, fuzz everywhere, and not one with a peach's blush. They were not delicate or sympathetic or brutal. They were just two big bullocks, one blond, one gray. But even they had a sense of the irony of the situation. Shows the higher class of cop the brutality stories are attracting these days.

The young one drove; Old Folk led the conversation.

Their big decision was whether they could book me as a Peeping Tom. I had been caught photographing another man's pornography. Old Folk looked back into the cage and drooled, "I ain't never had one just like you before, buddy. You do a lot of this sort of thing in my territory or you just started lately?"

"Go claim your pension," I suggested.

"Tough guy," he said, turning back to stare at the 11 p.m. traffic. "Tough guy. Wonder what he does for kicks."

The booking sergeant was in a surly mood. His wife must have kicked him in the balls as he left home for the night shift.

Of course I wasn't feeling any too pleasant myself. I was desperate for my film.

"You bastards are the scum of the earth," said Numb Nuts, hissing after my captors had delivered me and described my offenses. While I stood by they held a cop conclave and decided on "breaking and entering" and "invasion of privacy" as offenses, and "you fucking pervert" as a description of the captive.

But Numb Nuts really cheered me up. "Wait till you hear my name," I said, "then you'll really like me."

"What's your name?" he growled.

"Donald Duck," I said. "Honest. I was born in 1932 and my parents liked the alliteration."

"The allewhat? Fuck. Lock the bastard up."

"Hey, what about my call? I get a call."

"Call some of the guys downstairs. They're your kind."

Things were getting a little out of hand. I half expected a night on the city, but I didn't want to spend it with no machinery working for me. "Now look, I'm sorry if I offended you," you big shit. "But if you lock me up without a call, these kind gentlemen who brought me in aren't going to get their conviction. They can tell you. Or is Miller in? Jerry Miller. He can tell you my name. He's on tonight, ain't he?"

He squinted at me. "You know Miller? He knows you?" Spittle sploshed on floorboards behind the desk. "Figures. OK, you guys," to my arresting officers, "take him down the hall to the nigra."

Jerry Miller was a high school classmate of mine. He is also sergeant of police. I will never forgive him for showing no surprise at seeing me brought into his cubbyhole.

He was churning out some paperwork. They sat me down on a chair in front of him and flopped my file on his desk, and left. Jerry doodled a bit, then, without looking up again he picked up my file and skimmed it.

"Big bust like this," he said. "Wish I was in on it."

"This place smells," I said.

"Would have been promotion for sure. Want a smoke?"

"Screw your smoke." He knows I don't smoke. "I want to get out of here. I have an appointment in half an hour."

"Ah, we get them all here. Murderers, rapists, litterbugs, trespassers." He basked in it as we both remembered the hard times I have, on occasion, given him about being stuck for nine years as a sergeant. Think of it this way, he says, I've got more seniority than any other sergeant on the whole stinking force.

"Donald Duck, eh? No ID. I take it you expected to get caught."

"Not expected. It's a matter of protection, just in case. I've never been booked under my real name. Not since I was a kid. It helps out the license."

"Not so sure about the license on this one. What the hell are you up to anyway?"

"I'm trying to find out some secrets."

"Secrets of anatomy?"

"Secrets of the guy who rents that office. Very deep, very dark."

"Sounds right up my line."

We exchanged smiles. I was not in a bad mood considering my recent past and the prospects for my immediate future.

"Still on nights, I see."

"Yeah. It beats a beat. But it's not the easiest side of life. I get all the jobs that have filtered through everybody else and that nobody wants. Never any chance for anything big. I'm going to be here forever, unless I stumble onto something big by accident. Like, you know, drugs in a ski pole or something."

"Or in a stool leg," I said.

His face turned sharp. "What do you know about a stool?"

I sighed. "You don't have that one, do you?"

He got up and went to a cupboard. And brought back a very familiar-looking stool. "Somebody left a calling card in a north-side doctor's record room."

"I've never seen that stool before in my life."

"No drugs taken, nothing stolen. No fingerprints. We tell him to try and relax. Oh, I get all the trespassing cases."

"I've never seen that stool before in my life," I said. "But I could use one, when it gets unclaimed. Keep me in mind."

He sat down and shook his head. More for himself than for me. He propped up my booking sheet. "So what are we going to do about this? You going to tell me anything true so I can make like I beat it out of you and raise my standing around here?"

"Who rents the office?"

"Guy called Ames, according to the night watchman. That the guy you're working on?"

"Guess so. Give them my real name, and get me a phone call."

"That all you want me to do?" I was made the object of the bitter blade of irony. I spat it back; I thrive on irony.

"No. I want information. I want the Army records of a Leander Crystal and any Ames, Iowa, police record he has. You got that name?"

"I got it. You're sure I can't do anything else for you?" I sensed sarcasm but ignored it.

"If you can't get me out now, call my mother and ask her to bail me out tomorrow morning."

If it hadn't been his own office, he would have spat at my foot. Miller is a good spitter. "Now think carefully," he said. "Sure there's nothing else I can do for you?"

So I sat back and thought. "Also Army records of Windom, Sellman and Joshua Graham." I wanted to see if Crystal really was in the same

96

outfit as Joshua. "Let me write those names down for you." I wrote them down. He waited patiently. On reflection I think he was interested.

"Care to tell me what's going on?"

"No."

"Care to tell me what I'm going to get out of this? You know I can't just walk in and order Army records without some sort of reason."

"I may get you a fraud. And anything I do get will be yours."

"Such great temptations you offer." He sighed. "Still, it'll be interesting to see if anybody does notice what I'm asking for."

"I also need that film I took tonight."

"I figured that. You can't have it."

"I've got to have it."

"I'll see what I can do. But don't count on it."

I left quietly. For my night's rest.

By 1 a.m. I was making my one call. Privilege finally granted by Numb Nuts, the desk sergeant. I was getting pretty annoyed. Miller had identified me for them but his shift finished a little after midnight. I hadn't been caught doing violence. I thought they could let me go on my own recognizance. Numb Nuts wasn't buying any.

In return for his avowed failure to trust me—despite Miller vouching for me—Numbie decided that with one phone call I could hardly do a lasting damage to the community. So he gave me his phone. It was hard for him, I'll say that. He didn't want to see me go.

Which was handing me a problem. I could count on bail in the morning, but I could hardly expect my mother to come running down to the pokey in the middle of the night. When a kid is thirty-seven a mother's affection will only carry her so far.

I could call my lawyer, but I didn't have anything to say that couldn't wait.

So I resigned myself to a night courtesy of the city. I don't like bail bondsmen's breaths, or their 10 percent fee, which I didn't have on me, anyway.

Which left me with my phone call, which I damn well wasn't going to waste. I decided to use it on my next most pressing need—nights are pretty long in jail.

"Do you have a phone book?" I asked my cheerful bobby.

"Shit," he said, "you mean a bird like you don't know his mouthpiece's phone number by heart."

I shuddered as he handed me the book. There was something about his turn of phrase. An old movie word like "mouthpiece" put so close to a touching first-grade notion like "by heart."

I opened the book. The police department and the jail across the street are in my territory. They're walking distance from home. I know the area. I looked up my local all-night Chuck-a-Chunk-a-Chicken, dialed the number and took a breath.

"Would you please deliver a whole chicken and an order of french fries to the City Jail, please. The name is Duck, D. Duck."

It blew Numbie's mind. He clobbered me with the back of his paw; he gave me the look reserved for people who defile his phone.

I laughed, inside, all the way across the street.

Jail is not exactly a homey place, but if you know what to expect and have a degree of emotional reserve a night or two isn't that disorienting. I do recommend that you sleep as much as you can. It's without doubt the fastest way to pass time.

It's not exactly the first time I'd been in the Indianapolis jail. But I hadn't been there recently. It hadn't changed a bit. They still needed to arrest a decorator.

I never got my chicken.

21

Miller made a special trip in for me about ten thirty. That was the nicest thing anybody had done for me in quite a while. It meant that he hadn't forgotten me.

He was in high school with me, in my class. But I never met him until near the end of the summer after we graduated. One Saturday I had nicked a convertible from a Broad Ripple parking lot after a movie at the Vogue. I was heading out Westfield Boulevard going no place in particular and I recognized him hitching. I knew I'd seen him somewhere. So I stopped and picked him up. He'd been going to watch a baseball game at North Central. We got to talking. He had to pitch against one of the teams in a few days and he didn't have anything else to do.

We learned that we had some interests in common. Like exploring foreign neighborhoods.

We decided to take a ride. We drove that damn car about a hundred and fifty miles. Up to Kokomo and through Muncie, all around the northeast of town until we ran out of gas just outside of Oaklandon. From Oaklandon we walked back to the city. Ten miles. That sort of thing does something to a couple of people. No matter how different you are when you meet, and what ways you go after you part, you have a community of feeling that you never forget.

He had called my mother for me and when I was called in she'd already been and gone leaving the five-hundred-dollar bail.

I was in Miller's office by eleven forty five.

He gave me a fat manila envelope full of pictures. Prints from the rolls I popped the night before. "I've been reviewing your case," he said. "I think you may need these to prepare a proper defense."

I smiled. "Bet the lab loved this."

"It kept them out of trouble last night. They get horny if they just sit around and read Shakespeare all night."

We had a little more chatter and then he told me about Crystal's lawyer. "That guy, Ames. His lawyer's apparently been around here all morning finding out whatever he can."

"What'd he find out?"

"Finally, your name. Not much else that he didn't know. When you were caught, doing what. He wants the pictures and he's talking tough about prosecution. By the way they've added possession of burglar's tools to your charge sheet. Thought you'd like to know. They picked up your car in that shopping center. It's in the pound. You'll owe thirty bucks towing charges plus a parking ticket for leaving it there overnight."

I shrugged it off. I wanted to get going, but I'd had a night to think on my experiences. "Something else. Can you tell me what the problem is with the desk sergeant who was on last night?"

"Yeah. His old lady split the sheet with him. Took off. After twenty-three years. He doesn't know where. Every night when he comes on he checks at missing persons."

"Kind of rough on the people he books."

"Yeah, but it's kind of rough on him too." All heart, that Miller, too soft to make it against the odds. But a good man. I would still have trouble gleaning myself for sympathy for the sad-sack sergeant.

"You better go," he said. "I got to get home. I don't go on duty till four, you know."

"I know," I said. And I knew.

22

With no money in pocket, I decided to walk home and let the car ride. I stopped at my bank and convinced them to let me use one of their checks to draw out a little of my own money.

I took a hundred. Car money, when I got around to it, plus a little mad money.

Then I bought the highest-power hand magnifying glass I could find quickly, and I picked up a whole chicken with a double order of french fries. In the office, I made a call to make an appointment with my "mouthpiece" for four.

I ate my chicken. But I just stuffed it in. I was eager to get to the pictures that I had braved the bedbugs for.

Thirteen and a half rolls. Thirty-six negatives to the roll. Two or more pages pictured on each negative. My manila envelope contained prints of four hundred and ninety-one negatives, images of more than twelve hundred sides of pieces of paper.

I cut the prints up, so I had each photographed item separate. I set about arranging them in piles.

By three I had ten stacks of surreptitious snaps.

> Scrapbook
> Pornography
> Money
> Letters
> Canceled checks
> Tax records
> Ladies' names and phone numbers

Legal documents and bills
Accounting record book
Leftovers

I also had my first rewards. Four canceled checks dated from 1954 to 1956. Totaling twenty thousand dollars. Made out to a Jacques Chaulet; cashed, as well as I could make out, at a bank in Toulon.

I noticed the first one because of the French name. The others just followed. Not that I knew exactly what they meant, but they made me feel great.

Great enough to leave a note for Eloise:

Sorry to be gone today, but it's a good sign: I am working. I think I have a key to your parentage. Will be back as soon as possible after four. Wait if you can.

I debated signing it "Love." I mean I did feel good. But I decided to save it.

I paid for the car without a single crack, but couldn't help noticing that it wouldn't be hard to steal some of the cars the cops had in their emporium. It's not that I steal cars all the time. But my father showed me how to start them without keys and five or six times in high school . . .

But not a single crack.

I headed for Clinton Grillo's.

We didn't spend very long on my position with the police. Only on the facts and essential strategy. None of the "Why did you do it?" stuff. That's not really law—so Senior doesn't bother much with it. In law, he says, you accept what appears to be the truth, combine it with what you want to be the truth and try to settle out of court. Besides I don't think the old man wants to know too much about me. He still thinks of me as Junior's disadvantaged friend.

Clinton Junior got pretty good grades when we were in high school and he went to Yale. But he never came back. I went to see his father when I first came back to Indianapolis; to tell him about his son who was selling computers in New York while I lived there. Now Clinton

Senior is my lawyer and kind of a friend. And he doesn't send me bills. I take him bottles of good booze.

In this case the strategy was to delay. The longer we could stall "this guy Ames" the less likely he was to be upset and want to take the trouble to keep up prosecution.

Fair enough.

I also used the meeting to find out that the statute of limitations on inheritance fraud is six years in Indiana.

Happiness is a relative thing, of course, but as I headed back to my office I was happier than I'd been in some time. In work like mine, in which so much is so dull, you become afraid that your mind becomes dull with it.

Having gotten an unusual job I was pleased to have made progress. To have beaten part of it, if my guesses were correct. To have earned the fee by a little application, and a little daring, however inept. I didn't worry too much about being jailed. I have a fair number of friends in the city and they can help if you're not too important. Which I'm not.

I whistled in the car as I drove back.

I walked up the stairs rather than wait for the elevator. And I almost never walk up the stairs.

My only shadow was that for some reason Eloise had not been able to hang around. I thought that the note would be enough to keep her. I was glad I'd left such a positive one. I'd hurried back, so I was approaching the office door by 4:45.

I could see the door ajar. When I saw that my heart fluttered a little, as hearts will. That surprised me. I was, after all, an old man who was supposed to have better self-control than that.

I shook my head in wonderment at myself. I smiled, I strode into my office.

Sitting on the corner of my desk, with my note to Eloise in his hand, was Leander Crystal.

The sight cut me dead. I just stood there and started to shake. I don't know if he could see that.

After a minute's silence, I mumbled, "I need a drink," and tried to figure out how to get to my desk drawer. It shouldn't have been hard—I can see that now. But the sight of him there, where my Eloise, my client, should have been, it frightened me.

102

It took me another full sixty seconds to realize that I was in no immediate physical danger; he had no gun and he wasn't holding it on me. I was sure he knew I was shaking. I wanted him out. I wanted him away. We knew that we were enemies.

I said, "Get off my desk."

He got off and stood by the chair. Eloise's chair. I went behind my desk, sat down and did my thing. I went through three drawers before I found the bottle. The seal seemed inordinately strong. I can't say I felt better after the belt. It's just the only thing available to do. I don't take surprises very well.

"You expected my daughter, I believe." He spaced the words, enunciated clearly. Mr. Cool. "I sent her home. The poor child was very agitated. The surprise of seeing me. I must say I was surprised at seeing her here. But I decided to stay so that we could talk."

"I'm not sure that we have much to say to one another," I said, because it was my turn to talk and I am instinctively polite.

"I think this note you left for my daughter suggests the contrary."

"Ah, the note."

"Just what do you know about Eloise's parentage, Mr. Samson?"

"I'm still working on how you got here."

He shifted impatiently, and then decided to sit down. "You did break into my office last night. I have an unlisted phone number which I gave the night watchman to use in case anything suspicious goes on at the office. Your activities were deemed suspicious. I got your name from the police. I must say, I'm fascinated by the lengths to which you go for an article. But we'll drop that little fiction for the moment, shall we? You are a private detective, thirty-seven years old, originally of this city. You went away to college but dropped out when your father died. He was a guard at Marion County Jail. After some security work you went back to college, flunked out, wrote a book about your "experience" which was something of a *cause célèbre*. You married above you, had a daughter and dropped out of that because the pressure was more than you could take. Seven years ago you came back here, took out a detective license and have been living off that and other varied ventures. Your mother is alive and runs Bud's Dugout. She owns it outright. I presume on money you had left from your better days. I came here today to find out what you were doing in my office last night."

"Your secret office," I said, and then felt petty.

"My secret office. But I think your note told me that. I also wanted to know who put you up to it, and Eloise told me that. Now I want to know what you know. You can tell me that."

"Can I?" I was trying desperately to regroup.

"Don't try to play with the privacy of your client. Eloise gives you her permission to speak. Quite apart from the fact that she is a minor and I am her father. What, I repeat, what is it that you presume to know?" He was losing patience. I decided to give him one of the versions which fit the things I knew.

"I know that you are not her real father. I know she was conceived in France, and I believe her father was a man called Jacques Chaulet to whom you payed twenty thousand dollars for the service."

It stunned him slightly, but he was quick.

"Why would I do that?"

"In order that you and your wife inherit under the terms of Estes Graham's will, which required you to have a healthy child in wedlock. I believe you found out that you were sterile." It was worth a try, under the circumstances.

We paused together, studied each other intently. It was the kind of moment which someone interrupting us would have found comical. We did not find it comical.

I was waiting for him to speak. He, it turned out, for me. "Go on," he said.

Go on? I wished I could. He was only telling me what I already knew—that there was more. But I figured what I had given him was enough to get some attention. It had to be. Didn't it? I was almost glad he'd come.

I played it cool. "What else do I need? All I can add is that a copy of this information and instructions on how to use it are in a safe place, so don't get any ideas."

At this his eyebrows went up, creating seven wrinkles across his extensive forehead. He sighed the sigh of a rich man for dumb hired help. "If you think that I would harm you over a question of silence or a matter of money, you are the victim of delusions about your profession."

A put-down, but it worked. He made me feel foolish for feeling danger. But what the hell, it was my office and my chair.

104

There was another, though shorter, pause, after which he got up. "OK," he said, "please give this project a rest for the day. You will hear from me." And he walked out. With the walk of an assured man who knew what he wanted, knew how to get it and knew how to hang onto it. Everything I lacked.

Two hours of sitting later, and no booze, I had some idea of what happened. Of why I felt near death.

I had been futzing around in my own delusionary little world. I had accidentally locked bumpers with the real world, and the kind gentleman had come around to help straighten me out.

I had thought I was pretty big stuff. I had thought I was on the verge of the big time. Now I didn't feel I was anything.

I had met the enemy head on and I was his. I had accepted his terms. I had told him what I thought I knew; I had tacitly agreed to await his bidding.

He had said there was no danger for me. All he had done was say it, and I had accepted it.

I mean, what kind of turn of events was this for a self-respecting man?

Which brought up the larger question of whether I was, in fact, a self-respecting man.

The only thing that I wasn't sure of was that just because he said so, I had Eloise's permission to tell him the things I had already told him. That worried me too. That I had, with no hesitation, abandoned the discretion my client was entitled to. The discretion that I am legally obliged to give a client according to the Detective Laws of the State of Indiana which prohibit us from telling anything to anybody without authorization of client—except to police about crimes.

There was some excuse. It had been after the very first shock of his presence. But I didn't feel right about it. Two hours later, I decided to take some wild action. Strike back.

I dialed the Crystals' number. A man answered. I didn't recognize the voice. I asked for Eloise. There was a pause, some muffled talk and I was speaking again to Leander Crystal. I was sorely tempted to hang up on him, but that seemed unduly childish, even to me.

"Is that you, Samson?"

"It is I," said I.

105

"I'm sorry, but Eloise can't come to the phone at the moment. I was going to call you. Can you come to the house tomorrow morning around eleven? I'd like to straighten this situation out."

"I can be there. Will Eloise be there?"

"You will be able to talk to her then." And then he asked a question. "Your relationship with my daughter, it isn't anything that it, well, shouldn't be, is it?" Downright fatherly.

I drew myself up to my full telephone height. "Mr. Crystal. My relationship with Eloise is that of client and detective. I call her now because I am not convinced that I should have told you today what I did and I wanted to explain to her why I spoke to you. However if tomorrow we are to receive a full explication of this grimy situation then I believe her best interests will be served, and I will be satisfied. I shall be present tomorrow. Good-bye."

The thud of my hanging up reverberated through the hallowed halls of my office.

I felt rotten.

23

On a hunch I arrived at Crystal's house early, about nine o'clock. I'm not sure what I hoped to find—frenzied packing up and people running away—but it didn't pan out. I didn't see anything untoward.

On the other hand what I had simultaneously feared didn't take place either. That Crystal would spot my car down the street and come out and say, "If you insist on arriving early, then at least come in and wait where it's a bit warmer."

That happened to me once. One of the virtues of being small-time is that you don't have to have the same ethics that the big outfits have. You don't have to take every case that comes in, every old lady who wants her "boy" of thirty followed so she can get her hooks into the woman leading him astray this time.

And you don't have to play each case exactly straight. You can give personal service. The time I am thinking of, a wife hired me to get some divorcing evidence, if there was any, on her husband.

It was winter and I'd been sitting outside his girlfriend's house all night. By seven I was almost asleep and almost frozen when I looked up and the guy was tapping on my window. I didn't see him come out of the house. Maybe he saved me from freezing to death. I rolled down the window and he said to me, just like that, "If you're going to wait for me, you might as well come in where it's warm and have a cup of coffee."

So I did. We got to talking. And I failed to find evidence of any transgression for his wife. I told her how hardworking he was—he sells auto parts on Illinois Avenue—all those late nights alone at the store. I made it good. She almost believed me. I let her pay me, of course. After all, it was his money.

I still get my auto parts at cost.

Now an operative for a big agency couldn't work like that, couldn't afford to jeopardize the outfit's reputation.

But I've got no reputation that that sort of thing can hurt. Being small-time makes it much easier to play God, if you're so inclined.

Much easier to get your ego stomped too, but that's the other side of the coin.

At eleven o'clock, promptly, I rang the Crystal bell.

At eleven o'clock, promptly, Leander Crystal opened the door and ushered me into the living room from which he had so expertly ushered me in the recent past.

Eloise was there, sitting on a chair by the French doors. She was not the Eloise I had come to know. She was pale and tired and carried two bloodshot eyes. But her face was fixed in a kind of placid expression that it had never borne in my presence before.

Her father was a contrast. Ever the well-cared-for man of fifty, his eyes were clear and his voice was strong. Still Mr. Cool. He stood. I sat on the couch, the same place I'd sat when I talked to Fleur. He faced me and made a speech.

"I have talked to the other principals in this business and we have decided that the proper thing is that you be told the whole story."

I just listened. Skeptical, of course, but no longer surprised by anything.

"We aren't happy to have to bring you into our confidence—endow you with the family secrets, as it were—but Eloise assures us that you are honest and, we trust, discreet. We know that you are reasonably capable." Gracious concession. It made me a little proud.

"You know that Fleur and I married in 1949. You may not know that it was a love match and still is. Not perfect, but human. Part of the imperfection was through the agency of Fleur's father. While he lived he tried to control Fleur's mind and spirit."

A former bouncer speaking ill of the dead? I shifted my position. I crossed my legs. He continued.

"After he was dead, he asserted his values through the terms of his will. As you know Fleur's inheritance was conditional on our marriage producing a child." I nodded gratuitously, as if in time to the rhythm of his enunciation.

"He spoke of this condition on the will frequently while he was alive. In my opinion, he tried to cause trouble with it." One correct guess: they had known about the will before Estes' death.

"Then, in 1952, I found out that I could not have children." Another one right.

"Learning this, Fleur and I arranged a trip to Europe. There a friend I made during the war contacted a French doctor, who impregnated Fleur by artificial insemination.

"Fleur became pregnant at the end of January. When all appeared normal, we returned to Indianapolis, and announced the good news.

"So there it is. You have uncovered an impropriety. But surely the moral questions involved are not simplistic. Of course avarice was involved, but it's not Fleur's fault that I am sterile, and any other course of action would have made her suffer a life-style much diminished from what her father had accustomed her to.

"A larger mistake remains, our lies about Eloise's parentage. But we love her; she is our daughter in every real sense of the term. There can be no question that we wanted her, and that we hated the deception. We thought it best not to tell her, but we were wrong. Our greatest sin was that we underestimated our daughter and overestimated our ability to hide things from her, things about which our emotions were very strong. We won't underestimate her again. I just hope it's not too late. She thinks not; we hope not.

"There remains then only one basic problem: you. I don't know what you would intend to do with this information. There is not much you could do with it. 'Justice' cannot be further served; you have uncovered our skeleton and satisfied your client's requirements. All you could do with the information is cause us some social trouble. But the onus of

108

the gossip would fall on Eloise, and not on us. And that would be doing her a grave injustice.

"I've thought the problem over. What I propose is this. We, as a family, would very much like to obtain your silence. I will drop all legal charges pending against you, and give you a check for fifty thousand dollars. Both should be more than you would expect under other circumstances. In return, you will give back to me all records pertaining to this case, both those held by you and those which the police will return to you when I drop charges. And, naturally, we would expect your silence." At last he was silent; he was tired too. The whole business was costing him emotionally.

And it was a lot of money.

"May I ask you a question?"

"Of course."

"How does what you've told me square against your wife's recent miscarriage?" I'd thought it would hit him a little—I mean I didn't think he knew I knew about that.

The man did rub his eyes. But he said, "Mr. Samson, my wife is not a well woman."

"Which means?"

"Which means there was no miscarriage."

"She's pregnant?"

"There was no pregnancy."

For the first time since he had begun to speak I shot a look at Eloise. Still pale but placid.

He said, "Eloise didn't know. Clearly there has been a great deal about us Eloise hasn't known." He sighed. "My wife has recently been obsessed with a fear that we are going to leave her. She has wanted to be pregnant again very badly. I have had treatments but.... Well, a few months ago she decided she was pregnant. She told Eloise. Her doctor and I cooperated. For as long as we could."

We stared at each other, man to man. I was feeling more and more out of place. The guy was either a great actor or....

But why be charitable? So maybe he was a great actor.

He made a rueful face, not exactly a smile. "You note that the 'miscarriage' was of 'twins'?"

I nodded.

"Well, I believe that was meant to represent the fertility treatments I

109

underwent for her. A little mixed up but not without method, wouldn't you say?"

I didn't say.

"Welcome to the family, Mr. Samson. I know this is a lot to absorb all at once. You will need time to decide. I suggest this. I give you the check and drop charges. When you deposit the check we will assume you have accepted these terms and will return the films the police will give you when the charges are dropped."

"You would want no other guarantee?"

He shrugged. "What guarantee can I have? A piece of paper signed by you does not seal your mouth. Eloise says you are trustworthy. We will have to trust her judgment. Just what we failed to trust before." He looked at her tenderly. I looked too and her expression seemed not to have changed from fatigued placidity.

"I've made some commitments—it may take a little time to get out of them."

"Mr. Samson, a beggar cannot choose. I am begging you to spare us the social upset of a scandal. I cannot force you to keep silence. Avoidance of scandal is worth a good deal to us. But nobody cares fifty thousand dollars worth about us, except us."

"It's not a matter of the money."

"Then all I can say is that I would appreciate your making up your mind and dispatching this business promptly."

"May I speak to Eloise alone?"

"Of course." He turned on his heel and left the room. Eloise, my client, my pale frail client. Former client. "Did you really get put in jail?" she asked.

"Yes." I appreciated her sympathy.

"I didn't expect you to do that." Her sympathy wasn't sympathy. It was a degree of revulsion. It hurt me. I do not consider myself sordid.

"You're not responsible for what I did or do. And if I hadn't, you would never have been treated to this explanation, you mustn't forget that."

"I won't. I'm sorry." We sat in silence.

Finally I said, "What about all this? Are you satisfied?"

"Yes," she said.

"No other information you want?"

"Not that I can think of."

110

"The other side of the coin, would you object if I went on a little longer? Object not as a client but as a person." She didn't accept the compromise.

"Yes," she said hotly. "Why should you go on? It's not your family, it's mine. I'm happy now, happier than I've been in . . . ever!" Then she added gratuitously, one might say childishly, "If it had been me, it would have been more like five thousand dollars. You better take it before he changes his mind."

"Perhaps you will be a better businessman than your father."

"Maybe I will." She turned away. I left before she turned back. I was afraid of seeing dollar signs in her eyes.

I went to the hall door and opened it for Leander Crystal. He was waiting for me, sitting on the stairs to the second floor. He smiled self-consciously and got up. It was the first time he had smiled at me. I liked it; it was human.

We went back into the living room where Eloise still sat. From his pocket he pulled a small piece of paper with blue lines on it.

"I said I'd give you this," he said, and the voice was noticeably tired.

I put it in my pocket without reading the numbers. I didn't want to look crass.

"If there are any more questions I can answer for you, things you feel you must know—"

He was interrupted as the door across the living room flew open, and Fleur Crystal appeared. The door through which she had disappeared in fear the last time I'd seen her.

No fear now. She balanced herself carefully, holding onto the door frame with one hand and surrounding a little glass with the other. The glass's contents might have been iced tea, but I didn't see any lemon.

"So there you are," she screamed. "You mother-fucking bastard!" She laughed. "Did he tell you? *Did he tell you?*"

Crystal went to her and tried to lead her back to wherever she had come from. She was not docile, but with his hands on her she did not quite resist.

"Please," she whined, "let *me* tell him!" Crystal shot a look at me and I recognized my cue. I headed for the living-room door and beyond it, the front door. I mastered the intricacies, but not before hearing another piercing screech. I left with the words "artificial insemination" ringing in my ears.

111

I was still glad Crystal had smiled at me. I understood him better now, and I knew he was tired, very tired.

So was I. I went home.

But I couldn't stay inside. It was a decent day. I carefully took my jacket off and without looking in the pocket put it at the very back of my closet. I took out some sneakers and spent the afternoon shooting baskets in Brookside Park. Later I concentrated very hard on not thinking about Crystals. I succeeded pretty well until about 2 a.m. One of those thinking nights, not a sleeping night. Everything I had suppressed came back at once, deep dark ramblings. They were fierce. They gave me an ache in my stomach, which, though not hunger, I tried to quieten with milk. I didn't have enough in. It took me quite a while to find an all-night grocery. Then I drank too much.

When I got back I threw up. Then I slept like a baby. Till one in the afternoon. Why not? I was rich. Wasn't I?

24

By the time I pulled myself out of bed, I'd finally figured out why I wasn't running full speed to deposit the check.

The basic problem, the thing which kept me from walking the block and a half to the bank, was the transgression on, the usurpation of, my professional pride.

I try to avoid false pride in life. But I've spent some seven years establishing what I do and how I go about it. It may be something akin to scratching and pecking, but if I didn't like what I do I wouldn't do it. So when someone steps in and does it for me—and I haven't asked—it doesn't go down like a chocolate malt.

There were other things I wasn't entirely satisfied about. Little inconsistencies—or possibilities of inconsistencies. The temptation to accept something as true because someone has told it to you is an occupational hazard in my line. To do something properly you've got to cross-check facts and try to see how implications play off against each other.

I missed the three o'clock closing for the bank.

* * *

At 3:28 I got a call from Miller at Police HQ. He had just come on duty.

"What's your trick?" he wanted to know. "That poky lawyer was here, dropped all charges and asked that all the film you shot be given to you."

"It was just a little misunderstanding. The night watchman mistook me for the night maid and didn't realize his mistake until after he jumped on my back. Then to make it look good he knocked me out and took lots of pictures."

"The negatives and a set of prints are here when you want them. Sorry, I can't chat. I'm on the verge of arresting a notorious trespasser." He hung up.

It was a cool but pleasant day. I took a walk to the police station.

On the way I passed three banks, all closed.

Miller played it cute all the way.

He left the film and prints for "Donald Duck." I was lucky—my boy Numb Nuts was on the desk and he pulled out the envelope as soon as he saw me.

But I had no time to stop and marvel.

The phone was ringing when I got back to the office. It wasn't Eloise. It wasn't anybody. It was a lawyer I work for asking if I would serve some papers for him. Without thinking I said no, that I was on a case. A concept which interested me, because it meant I was employing myself.

I read for a while. Around dinner time I decided that I couldn't go on with this "I will go on; I won't go on; I will cash the check, I won't cash the check" stuff.

As a bold stroke, I decided to let the whole matter stew for a few days.

During dinner, canned lamb stew, I reflected on the fact that I now had two sets of prints from the film, and I considered cashing the check, sending the negatives and one set of prints to Crystal, and working from the other set of prints anyway.

I rejected that as unprofessional.

After dinner I started looking over the pictures again.

Twelve hundred and forty-one of them. That didn't last long. It was just the sort of thing I hadn't done with the medical records. But what expert could I send these to?

113

Then I thought about the medical records and checking notes. I wondered who Fleur's doctor was, the new one after Fishman was dumped. I wondered if I should ask Crystal. He'd said I could.

But I decided definitely not to ask him. I either bought his story or I didn't.

I mailed a letter to New York City, asking for a copy of Eloise Crystal's birth certificate.

I considered asking my woman what I should do. I mean, what's a woman for? I went to see her on the way to mail a letter to New York. But it would have taken a lot of explaining to bring her up to date. I couldn't quite bring myself to force the explanation on her. What with the other things we had to talk about. Thanks to a great act of will, while I was with her the whole thing slipped my mind.

25

At eleven the next morning I was in the library. Looking up artificial insemination and sterility.

Britannica: "This is insemination of a breeding female by other than natural mating. . . . It was used long ago by the Arabs in horse breeding. Fowls, rabbits, dogs and other animals have been bred by artificial insemination. Beginning in 1940 the practice became widespread in the United States particularly with dairy cattle. . . . The semen may be collected in a number of ways. . . . In most stud bulls, the artificial vagina method . . . is preferred."

And on sterility: "Involuntary failure to reproduce (infertility) occurs in 10 percent of married couples in most populations that have been studied. . . .

"'He whose testicles are crushed or whose male member is cut off shall not enter the assembly of the Lord.' (Deuteronomy 23:1). . . .

"Correction of female infertility is more successful [than correction of male infertility]; mechanical problems can sometimes be corrected surgically and it is even possible to induce ovulation by giving human gonadotrophin. . . ."

Americana: ". . . A wife may be inseminated artificially with semen from a donor selected by a physician. This may be done when the husband is sterile or has an inheritable defect that he does not want to transmit to his children. The United Presbyterian Church in the U.S.A. in 1962 approved artificial insemination for couples with 'intelligence and emotional stability' and urged uniform state laws to protect the legal rights of 'test tube babies.'"

Stedman's Medical Dictionary: Nothing.

Collier's Encyclopedia: "Since about 1920, artificial insemination has been resorted to in many cases of sterility. . . The practice is not universally adoptable because of emotional and religious objections."

Which proved? The thing could have taken place exactly as advertised with regard to artificial insemination. I had hoped to find that nobody thought of artificial insemination for people till about 1956. Only thirty-five years out.

I wanted to prove I was being lied to. Because I don't like being lied to. Which would be incentive enough to go on with it all. Despite the respect I'd acquired for Leander Crystal I felt he *must* be lying to me. Basically because I didn't think what I knew was worth fifty thousand dollars, not even in scandal. I would have been more like Eloise. I might have settled for five thousand dollars.

What I would do was go on long enough to prove whether or not I had been lied to.

I would explore no new avenues. Go over notes, OK. Make visits to people I was already committed to visit. Check the records I had solicited from Miller and tell him what I had. Read my mail. And maybe have a look over the pictures I got from Crystal.

And if nothing came up, in a week, I would deposit my check and make a withdrawal and . . .

I went off for lunch at Joe's. In the middle of my second burger I nearly drowned in an urge to run to my nearest bank. What matter that it was Saturday. I would bang on the door until someone let me in. When I was going down for the third time, I ordered lemon meringue pie, chocolate ice cream, black coffee and decided to give it three days, max.

26

Mrs. Forebush was her old self. I wondered just what she did in that Fiftieth Street house. Whether she ever went out, how she got her food. The nearest grocery store is at Forty-ninth and Washington Boulevard, three goodly blocks away. On second thought, I figured she managed.

When we were seated in Indianapolis' Victorian Room I gave her the story as Crystal gave it to me. I had thought about trying to bowdlerize it, but decided that if fifty thousand dollars bought my silence, Eloise's welfare bought hers. I didn't mention Crystal's offer of cash.

When I finished she said, "Fleur never was what you call stable. I guess it all makes sense now." She was examining me with great care to see whether that was what I thought.

"I guess it does," I said and tried to examine her back.

"But I don't see the problem. The child was born in wedlock, and was Fleur's child, that is all that was required."

"It's maybe it was having told a lie without having any way to confess to it in the end," I said piously. "One thing that has happened to me, I have developed a considerable personal respect for Leander Crystal. He's an unusual man."

She nodded her head vigorously. "He owns this house, you know. He lets me live here rent free and gives me sort of a pension."

"You told me. When did you move in?"

"Almost as soon as poor Estes died. Fleur and Mr. Crystal went to New York two days after the funeral and he made arrangements for Red Bull Homes to have me moved here two days after that."

"Do you know when he bought the house?" I bought a house once; it was a lot of trouble.

"No, but it had been lived in. I think he kicked the tenants out or at least they left in a hurry. They left a lot of food and china and things like that. Woolworth-type china." She looked appraisingly at her own china display case. "See that flowered bowl. It's Minton, you know."

"It's very nice."

"And the food. Some of it was funny vegetables. Artichoke hearts and endives. But what can you expect from a foreigner? She was a foreigner, you know."

116

"No, I didn't know. How do you?" She looked at me sharply as if my words carried some sort of criticism, which I guess they did. Real Indiana people are not friendly to the notion of foreigners. People from the bordering states—Illinois, Michigan, Ohio and Kentucky—might be relatives. But other states they hesitate over. Foreign countries are just another world when they are convinced that their Indiana world is the best one.

I once traveled through Indiana with a man from England who was "doing" the whole country, collecting Americana. We stopped briefly at the old James Whitcomb Riley house on Route 40.

Everybody who goes to school in Indiana learns about James Whitcomb Riley.

We thought to buy postcards and when we took them to the cashier the lady listened to my friend and said, "You a furriner?"

He did a double take and nodded. "Guess I better report you to the police," she said.

We both did double takes and after an hour-long ten seconds she gave a half smile and said, "I was just kidding. Hope you have a real nice trip." The trip did get nicer.

With Mrs. Forebush I had let my prejudice against Indiana's prejudice get the better of me.

"I know she was a foreigner, young man. I ought to know. There was an Immigration Department man who came here every June for five years asking about her. Started in 1955. He said she hadn't registered in January like aliens have to. And that this was her last known address. I remember him because each year the same man came around asking the same questions. Each year it was as if I'd never spoken a word to him the year before. Sometimes I wonder what the written word is for. Couldn't they have made a note on her card or something? Then one year he stopped coming. I guess they found her."

"I guess."

"But Mr. Crystal has been very good to me." She said it in that way which indicates that a conversation is nearly over.

"The only other thing I wanted to ask you, Mrs. Forebush, it may be on the personal side, but I wondered. When I talked to Fleur she said that you'd had hopes of marrying Estes Graham someday."

She grew a bit sad, but no longer bored. "I don't really know that I should talk about this to you. My relationship with Estes Graham was an unspoken thing, a lovely thing. I guess I did expect to marry him at one point. I would have begun to think of it about the beginning of the war, three years after Irene died. He was a man consumed with his own energy, a vibrant man, even then, and he was seventy years old when the war began. But when the children began to die he did too. First Windom in 1942, then Slugger—that was the second son, Sellman—when he died in 1944 we both just knew that he would never marry again. Then when Little Joshua went it just crumpled him up. One day he called me in and told me he had put a hundred thousand dollars worth of stocks in my name so that if he died, I would be taken care of.

"A few weeks later he had a stroke. I think he expected to die, not too long after that. Maybe if the youngest child, Fleur, had been a boy things would have been different.

"In 1946 Mr. Crystal came to Indianapolis to go to Butler and get his college degree on the GI Bill. And as soon as he arrived he called on Estes. He was a friend of Joshie's in the war, you know. And when Mr. Crystal started showing some interest in Fleur, well . . . I think Leander Crystal is responsible for Estes' living another six or eight years.

"I don't know many young people. And there will never be another Estes Graham. But the only one I know who ever came close was Leander Crystal." She paused for a moment. And looked at me with a wetness in her eyes. "I always sort of thought of Eloise specially. As if she were the child I might once have had."

The rest of Fleur's accusations I let go.

We parted with our understanding intact—and even expanded to contain a degree of mutual admiration for Leander Crystal.

When I got back to my office it was pushing four. With a degree of nostalgia I decided to make myself a pot of tea, for teatime.

The nostalgia was more than for Mrs. Forebush's Victorian perspicacity. It was in memory of clients gone by. Four o'clock was Eloise time for me. I set and wound the cuckoo clock.

The little bird came at four, but not Eloise.

Eloise, my Eloise. My million-dollar client. My million-dollar baby. Why is money so corrupting? Because I guess one expects to be corrupted by it. I was glad it was after three. Another day gone by safely. I didn't intend to deposit the check for at least two more days but . . . .

The notion of having, sometime, to tell the story of how I let fifty thousand dollars get away just by being slow to deposit really hurt.

Think of telling Maude. She'd never forgive me. I thought how an upholstered chair in the office would be a lot less likely to show the dust.

But I cut myself off. If I went on like that, exaggerated to myself, I would be in debt before the banks opened in the morning. Keep busy, I said to myself. Keep busy. Keep what portion of your mind is operable busy.

In my second mug of tea, instead of adding milk, I added bourbon. It grows hair, I figured; would make me strong. And I dialed Jerry Miller.

When I got through to him he told me he had some things for me.

I was feeling a little giddy. I asked him when he ate, and invited him out to dinner at Cappy's.

"What's the matter with you, find ten bucks in the street and want to see how fast it'll go?"

"It was eleven dollars and thirty-two cents, but I think it's counterfeit. You coming or do I have to go down there and try to get through my friendly desk sergeant?"

"At eight," he said. And then he added, "Got to go now, there's been this rash of trespassers," and he hung up, so I knew he loved me.

Between four thirty and setting off by foot for Cappy's I wrote a letter to my daughter, and spent between a hundred and sixty and a hundred and eighty thousand dollars.

My man Miller is not, basically, a happy man. He's married to his second choice, for instance. When we came out of high school he was in love with this girl who was highly lovable and who loved him and wanted to marry him. That was the problem—he wanted to go to cop school and she didn't want to wait.

So she married a musician and turned him into a suit salesman and lived happily ever after.

Not that Jerry's wife—it's been almost twenty years now—is not a fine wifely specimen. But somehow he's never quite made it where he wanted to make it.

I understand his problems.

We settled down to dinner and he gave me a folder. I set it aside and didn't look at it through the whole meal.

119

"I'm sorry I haven't got anything to trade you for this," I said. I was sorry. I felt fairly bad about it.

"But you've been digging around with these people?" He tapped the folder by my salad plate.

"Not digging uninvited. I was hired by one."

"But you found something."

"The way it stacks now I maybe did. But the friendly people from the statute of limitations have cut out anything there might have been."

He tapped the folder again. "You're under arrest. Obtaining information by promising me a fraud and then not delivering. That's fraud." In our younger days at such a moment he would have pulled out his cuffs and slapped them on me. But we've both mellowed, and we just sat in silence and thought about things.

"The best I can do is offer to confess to trespassing. But I won't unless you promise to give my stool back."

"The hell of it is," he said, "when I requested those records nobody turned a whisker. I think I could file for a Washington police report on the President and nobody here would notice. I must be the most experienced sergeant on the whole force. And what do I get?"

"Night shift," I said. "Probably nobody notices anything that night shift puts in."

"Aw shit," he said. "Al, do you make any money in that racket of yours?"

I must have blushed. He was hitting very close to home. "Sometimes," I said, "but not very often. I was thinking of asking you the same question."

"There must be something better that we can do. Some way to get along without taking all the crap we take. If I had some money I'd throw in with an uncle of Janie's. He's got him a lake down in Kentucky that he's working up into a resort. You know, motorboats and fishing and special buses to the Kentucky Derby."

"You gotta offer free coffee, year round. So people will come out of season."

"I'm not kidding, Al."

"Neither am I. Why don't you become corrupt for a few years to build your stake?"

"Nobody ever offers me anything."

"I'll give you five bucks for my stool and a guarantee nobody will raid my joint at three in the morning."

He gave an involuntary bristle. He can't help it. He's mellowed some but he's basically an honest cop. That's the real reason he doesn't get on. Not because he's black but because he's so bloody self-righteous about his business. A long time ago I considered trying to act as go-between with him and Maude. She could have used an ear at HQ. But it wouldn't have gone. What he does occasionally for me as a friend, he never would have done for money on a committed basis. Maude wouldn't have paid that much anyway, and now she has an ear a little closer to the mainstream.

Daydreams of little country cottages with gardens filled out our chow.

At the end I reached for the check and he reached for the folder of information.

"Hey," I said, and I grabbed for it too. We stood there each with a hand on the folder.

"Thought you said you were off it."

"Well, I don't have a client anymore, but I'm giving it another day or two. . . ."

"You've either got it bad, or you're not telling me everything."

"Or both," I said. We let it go at that.

27

I walked home pretty quickly. That's fair enough. A fellow's entitled to walk at any speed he wants, isn't he?

So I had it bad. So? So. I clutched the records Miller gave me to my bosom. So? So maybe I was just looking for enough to justify cashing in on what was available. So maybe this and maybe that. So maybe I just have an irrational need to check and cross-check.

Home; stairs; office; bourbon; glass (!); dining-room chair.

The police file was on top. Ames, Iowa. Surprisingly Leander Crystal had a police record. Picked up twice in 1939 the first time for grand theft auto (charges dropped). The second time for petty theft. "Charges dismissed when subject agreed to join the Army."

So the missing year was filled in. Born 1920. Graduated from high school in 1938. Interesting in itself, that he had been able to stay in school. Joined Army in 1940. Intervening year: bum. Motivation for enlistment: better than jail.

And it had been. The Army can serve some excellent social functions. Apart from reducing population.

It was hard to believe that the exceptional man I knew as Eloise's father had started that way. Time and tenaciousness.

And we had something in common. We had both pinched cars—but I was never caught. It made me feel smug.

Crystal's Army records indicated that he had had an active and heroic fighting career in which he was twice decorated, which I knew. At the end of the war he had been on supply duty in southern France, which I hadn't known.

There were indications from various of his superiors that Crystal had expressed interest in an Army career. In fact the only blot on his record happened in basic training. Someone had accused him of fathering her child. Suit was initiated, but "the claim, contested by the soldier, was subsequently dropped." He had been shipped out of Europe shortly thereafter.

No further claims of that sort had been made during his stay in the Army. Had he but known then what he knew now.

As a matter of fact, that happened to Bud when he was in. He was an MP in London in World War I and a lady purported that her impending child shared a father with me. And she dropped the claim too, after a miscarriage. I guess it can happen to anyone.

I had a drink and waxed ironic.

I took the Army records of Sellman and Windom Graham. I'd asked for them for completeness—more to annoy than to edify.

Good soldiers, brave soldiers, dead soldiers.

Joshua Graham I studied.

He had enlisted late for the war, but early for a man, shortly after his eighteenth birthday. He had finished high school and joined. He got to Europe in December, 1944, celebrated his nineteenth birthday in March of 1945 and was killed in August when a supply truck he was driving

122

detonated a previously undiscovered German mine. The Army adjudged the death accidental.

The story as reported in the Army records was identical to that which Leander Crystal had written to Estes.

My main inquiry was satisfied. Crystal had been in the same Army administrative unit as Joshua had. Fact as advertised. Moreover, Joshua had worked under Crystal in supply.

I checked my notes and went on further in Joshua's file. The only thing that did not check was Leander's claim that he had been on the scene and had heard Joshua's last words. According to the Army's records there had been a man on the scene, a witness who had been by Joshua's side when he died. A doctor, the doctor who had later certified Joshua's death. A Henry Chivian.

But Leander had written the Grahams and taken the witness's place. I found that interesting. That Leander had seen fit to place himself by Joshua's side. It seemed quite a step from the Iowa petty burglar, from the daring hero.

It represented planning ahead. What else could it mean? Leander had spotted Joshua and had identified him as the son of a rich man. He had befriended the boy, so obviously unsoldierly. Probably gone out of his way to befriend him. And when he died, rather than let this friendship's potential die too, Leander had laid the groundwork for arriving in Indianapolis to make himself a place in the world of the Grahams.

"Educational plans." Had he known ahead that Joshua had a sister? Had he decided to court her while pondering what Joshua's death would do to his prospects?

It was a little extra dimension to Leander Crystal, husband in a "love match." Perhaps having fought as a man who didn't worry about death, he had made the transition. The man with a master plan. Maybe he had learned to love life while he had it.

He had come a long way.

I paused to refill my glass and I looked back over Joshie's records. I looked again at the real witness's name. Dr. Henry Chivian.

I consulted my notes, and found where I had seen it before. There it was: Dr. Henry Chivian, the man who had certified Estes Graham's death ten years and five thousand miles later.

Another irony. I bourboned ironic again. And after a while I just bourboned.

Saturday is not the best night of my week.

I stayed conscious deep enough into the a.m. to see the Pacers lose to the Utah Stars on television, but the telecast was not the only reason I slept past Sunday morning.

The afternoon I spent with my woman and her daughter.

28

Monday morning brought business. A nine o'clock call to serve a stack of subpoenas. For some reason I said yes and by ten I was on the trot.

I guess I was trying to get away a little. Sure I was still on the Crystals and the Grahams, but I wasn't happy about it.

Basically because the drift seemed to be away from the fifty thou, not toward it. I was so much happier when things looked like taking the money. Maybe I took the subpoenas so that I wouldn't succumb to the recurring urges to go and cash the check.

How could I stop at the bank if I was busy with subpoenas?

What was so special about me that I wouldn't take the money and run?

I guess just that I had some money once, and it's not all it's cracked up to be. Or maybe the thought of getting money again opened up the mental possibilities of getting some of the other things back again. Like my daughter.

At one I permitted myself to stop for lunch. By pie time it occurred to me that what had seemed so strange a couple of nights before was not all that strange. Dr. Chivian. What would really have been strange would be if his signature had appeared on death certifications in France and Indianapolis a week apart.

But ten years? It's a lot of time.

And it began to fit.

Suppose Crystal knew Chivian in France, as well as Joshua. Suppose Crystal and Chivian got along. Suppose, when Leander found he was sterile, or suspected it, he contacted Chivian to make the tests because he could count on Chivian's keeping the results quiet. It fit with the abrupt change of doctors which had shown up in Fleur and Leander's medical files. Chivian arrived and stayed on as their family doctor. And Chivian had happened to be around when Estes breathed his last.

Not bad for a guess.

No, not a guess; a deduction. Very classy.

After I paid for the eats I checked a phone book for a Henry Chivian, MD.

There was none. Not even a plain Henry Chivian.

You can't win them all.

I let it go. Till three, and two subpoenas filled the time.

By the time I got back to the office I was more or less resigned to starting on the kind of job I hate. Wading through the minutiae in all those pictures from Crystal's office. It was the only thing I could think of to find Chivian. I presumed that he was somewhere in the area, or at least had been some fifteen years before. Probably he still was, because Fleur and Leander had not returned the bestowal of their patienthood to Fishman, *fils*. They might just have gone to some other doctor entirely; certainly I had not found Wilmer Fishman the most charming individual I had ever encountered, though he still ranked above Numb Nuts. Still, Fishman was thriving and it was reasonable to assume that he had picked up enough bedside manner to retain his father's patients, all things being equal.

So I assumed Chivian was in the general area. Where? I could ask Leander. Or some other Crystal.

Scratch that. I prefer not to stir the fire under the foot until I have nothing else to do.

I could go to the library and go through phone book after phone book in the Indianapolis area. They have them. I could get as far away as Chicago, Detroit or Cincinnati that way. If you live near an airport there it can be faster to Our Town than driving from Evansville or Fort Wayne in the state. But leafing through phone books is highly inefficient.

So I gambled that there would be some record of Chivian in Crystal's records. Fair enough. One presumed that with Crystal the rich one, there would be some recorded flow of cash from Crystal to Chivian.

A pot of tea and an hour and a half later, I found it. The things that

125

take the greatest amount of time in this business are the ones that can be most easily summarized. "I studied the financial records until I found some checks made out to Henry Chivian, MD." A thing like that could stand for days of work; this can be the dullest job in the world.

But at least it's work you can do while listening to the radio. Like baseball, if there were any baseball on the radio in Indianapolis. The tenth largest city in the country, and no major-league baseball. Just the Indianapolis Indians, perpetual triple A farm club, community-owned. When I was younger, just out of college the second time, my mother bought me a share of Indians' stock, symbolic of her wish that I come home and settle down. But those were the days when I had major-league aspirations. 1956 it was, and the stock cost ten dollars. The next year I got a free ticket to a game as my dividend. Now, fourteen years later, I get memories. Since big-league basketball and the Pacers came to town I've become a basketball man. That Roger Brown!

A few minutes before five I found the series of checks paid to Henry Chivian. Two items of interest: first, that the recent ones were deposited in a Lafayette, Indiana, bank, which probably located him for me. "Recent" was from 1957. The ones before then were cashed or deposited in Indianapolis. The Chivian theory upheld.

Second, the checks were issued very regularly and since the move to Lafayette, they were sent twice a year. On the order of five thousand dollars in '57 growing to fifteen thousand dollars in 1970.

That could mean only one of several possible things. Unfortunately, I didn't know which one.

For instance, it was not a lot of money for someone to hit a man with Leander Crystal's resources for. If it were payment for covering up anything.

It was also not a large amount of money for a doctor to move to an area for, not if he had any class, and somehow I figured that to deal for so long with Crystal he had to have some class. But it was a nice annuity, and maybe he was an obliging, unambitious fellow.

Why did I assume that anyone dealing with Crystal had to be ambitious?

It also occurred to me that it might mean that someone in the Crystal household was a junkie. Fleur presumably.

And why Lafayette? Why not Indianapolis? Surely it's a big enough town to insure secrecy, if that's what was desired. Crystal had proved that in his "Ames" office. Of course the decision had been made in the late fifties, but Indianapolis was still pretty big then, over four hundred thousand. Maybe there was some nostalgia about the old days in France, and the name Lafayette.

I nearly thought myself past five o'clock. But not quite.

I got the phone, asked for and got Chivian's office number from Lafayette information and then dialed direct.

I got a very kindly voice saying, "Doctor Chivian's office." Very kindly. Like young and pretty and, well, kindly. I asked her for an appointment, which she correctly took to mean with the doctor.

"I can give you next Monday at two o'clock."

"I was hoping that I could have it sooner; I mean, would it be at all possible to squeeze me in tomorrow afternoon?"

"May I ask the nature of the problem you want to discuss with the doctor?"

"It's, well, it's a male problem."

"I understand." She understood! "If you can come in tomorrow at about two, we'll try not to keep you waiting too long. May I have your name and address please?"

I nearly blew it by calling myself Henry. "It's Harry, that is, Harrison Keindly." I spelled it for her. "But everybody calls me Harry."

"All right, Harry, you come in tomorrow around two. Thank you for calling."

Very kindly. Now and then, a voice just seems to do it for you. I spent dinner wondering what I should wear.

My postprandial preslumber period I spent very virtuously working in the office. Going through Crystal's tax records and bills. I picked up each photograph, studied each sheet through my magnifying glass and tried as hard as I could to figure out what the hell it could possibly mean.

I didn't do very well. My familiarity with the paper trappings of money is rudimentary. When I was involved in such things, for my brief period of affluence in the late fifties, I had a tax accountant to do all that stuff. I just signed. I was fighting the crowd I found myself running in, professional people of all sorts except finance who spent all their time talking about the manipulations of money. I fought them successfully; all the way home to Indianapolis. It's another reason I hesitated over starting to go through Crystal's stuff carefully. It sort of meant more to me than itself, but once started. . . .

I found three pieces of information I recognized. Deeds and purchase agreements to two properties and records of sale of a third.

The sale was the property "known as Graham House" on North Meridian Street. It brought the tidy bundle of $96,500 in August, 1955. At about the same time the house at 7019 Jefferson Boulevard was bought for $58,000.

The third property I was also familiar with, a house on Fiftieth Street on a 47- by 64-foot lot. Mrs. Forebush's house. Crystal bought it in September, 1953. He paid thirteen thousand dollars. That seemed high to me. Not far off what the house would bring now.

Attached to the deed were bills for adding an electric opener for the garage, landscaping to the extent of adding tall shrubs, and inside the house, cleaning it out, installing furniture, twin beds, and new locks on all doors.

Very ambitious. I could understand it, the deed and the improvements, I mean, if not exactly why. It occurred to me that Mrs. Forebush might have some wisdoms on the subject.

It also occurred to me that for several hours I had not given a thought to the fifty thousand dollars.

I was pouring a glass of orange juice when the phone rang. It was Leander Crystal. He did the talking.

"I'm sorry to bother you at this late hour, Mr. Samson, but I was thinking about you and it occurred to me that I might have overlooked something that might be worrying you. The matter of the check I gave you. If you would prefer, and I think you probably should, I can give you all or part of the money in cash."

"That's a lot of money to have lying around the house."

"I don't mean to be gross, Mr. Samson, but when there is a certain amount of capital around, such things can be done fairly easily."

"I see. I appreciate your telling me. That isn't what has been holding me up, though I probably would have got to it."

There was an intratelephonic pause. I sensed he wanted to speak and was trying to find the words. He found them. "Again, I don't mean to apply even the slightest pressure, but I wondered if I might be of any assistance in resolving whatever it is that *is* holding you up."

128

"Now it's my turn to want not to be gross, Mr. Crystal. But to be frank I have never been bought off a case before and I am the sort of person that I have to be absolutely certain that it is what I want to do."

"I see. In fact, the delay should be a comfort to me. It is a testimony to your scrupulousness. Well, shall I leave it at this? If you have any questions that I can help you with, or if you want to talk about the matter I called about, then call me."

"I shall."

"I just want you to know, Mr. Samson, I appreciate a man with scruples."

"So do I, Mr. Crystal."

I adjourned for the evening. I spent so long daydreaming about little cottages by Kentucky lakes and adjacent vegetables gardens and tax-free dollars that it took me until past one in the morning to understand that he was sweetening the pot by implying that my "scruples" might lead to subsequent employment and financial benefit.

By the time I got to wondering if he was a member of the Mafia I knew that I had hit bedtime. I mean, Fleur on drugs was one thing, but me becoming a gangland pawn was another.

29

Late to bed, and late to rise. I had sort of hoped to be able to take a few side trips. My mother's parents came from the territory between Lafayette and Indianapolis. Kokomo, but more specifically such metropolises as Camden and Deer "Crick" and Flora and Delphi. Where she grew up, Logansport was the big city. You know, where the city slickers come from.

But I had no time to stop and renew acquaintance with the land of my origins. I had to hustle to get to Chivian's Lafayette office by two.

His office was not merely an office, however. But a clinic with doctor's name riding high. One Crystal thing must have led to another. The cat was doing pretty well.

My golden-voiced secretary was a disappointment. I hadn't really thought she would be. I had prepared myself for a beast, or possibly, outside chance, a beauty. But no. Just an ordinary old Hoosier lady of about thirty. Definitely middle-of-the-road.

Until she spoke, of course, but I was a little too nervous to admire her vocal qualities. I had trouble following the things she said.

Like "Mr. Keindly?" It nearly threw me. It was not said with a great sense of recognition, and I had been thinking of other things.

So I nodded.

"Doctor will see you when he's finished with the patient he's with. Will you take a seat please? It'll only be a few minutes."

I was alone in a strange waiting room. Somehow one always expects to be sitting along with other people in a doctor's waiting room. I idled away the time with magazines. One has to be very careful about a doctor's magazines. They have the usual picture, entertainment and news publications sprinkled around, but the nitty gritty of the magazine budget goes for medical journals of various sorts which then do double duty in the waiting room. If you're not very careful you will pick up one of them and find yourself reading about the types of cancer commonly found in children and how little there is you can do about three-quarters of them. Not highly constructive for parents bringing kiddy-kid to see doc-doc about that lump-lump on his head.

Or for detectives who haven't seen their daughters for a long time. I go on record against cancer in children.

A very attractive brunette-type broad left what I presumed to be the doctor's chamber. She was about the same age as my secretary, but everything that I had hoped my secretary was going to be. As the door closed behind the brunette, I turned back to the lady at the desk. It gave me the opportunity and motivation to evaluate her face, the suntan makeup pancaked over the pimple scars.

Then our eyes met. An extraordinary thing happened. "As a matter of fact, they're from chicken pox I had when I was eighteen."

"I'm sorry," I said, and I was, terribly. "Would you come out with me tonight?"

She held up her left hand, a finger of which bore the answer to my question. Her intercom buzzed.

"I am a fool," I said.

"Yes," she said. "Doctor will see you now." The doctor's door opened and Henry Chivian strode out, right hand extended.

"Mr.—um, Keindly, I believe. I'm Doctor Chivian. Come in, won't you."

I came in. Chivian was average height, but with a dark, real tan, bushy eyebrows and a thick head of black hair. He moved back to his desk quickly, almost ruthlessly. There was something about him.

I spent a few moments looking around the office, a prosperous office of a modern cut, but with a medical degree framed at the right, in the position on the wall which is a medical compromise—where both patient and doctor can look at it. So I looked at it. University of Oklahoma, January, 1943. I didn't know by how much, but that made him older than Leander Crystal. He didn't look it.

The rest of the office, books on an open shelf, some cupboards, quite trim, and a few pictures on the top of the bookshelf, below the medical degree. One an Army picture, two others, both of the doctor with other men, apparently in distinguished settings. I couldn't quite make out what. But I didn't have a lot of time.

The doctor was looking businesslike. "Mrs. Rogers says that you have some sort of male problem, Mr. Keindly. That can cover a lot of ground."

"I want to be frank with you, Doctor. I didn't come to see you about myself. I have a rather delicate problem and I hoped that you could help me solve it."

His lips curled into a slight smile. Perhaps he liked delicate problems. He sat back, the better to enjoy. "Go on."

"I have a feeling you've guessed," I said, "but I'll say it anyway. My daughter has gotten herself in trouble, I mean pregnant. I hoped that you would help us or send us to someone who could."

"But why do you choose me to come to? Surely no one is going around saying that I do abortions." The trace of a smile remained in place. And I was getting information.

"No, but a friend of mine, well. . . . The thing is that we're pretty desperate. Lucy, that is, my daughter, left it kind of late to tell us about, and we don't really know much about this sort of thing. We never expected . . . that is, we spoke to a friend and she said that she didn't know but that you were a nice doctor, and that you might conceivably help us, or tell me where we could go to get help."

131

"How exactly did Lucy get herself in this kind of trouble?" He let the question dangle for a moment, wading in the implications. But he stepped out just as I was about to tell him about the hayride I unwisely let little Lucy go on in the spring. He said, "I mean, didn't Lucy know such a thing might happen, or is she the type of girl who is quite careless with her affections and her defenses?" Oh, he was enjoying it all right.

"I wouldn't say that," I said.

"Now, Mr. Keindly, surely you are a worldly enough man to have realized that nobody's daughter is safe in this world of the flesh, surely not without education, preparation and warning. Surely you could at least have shown her how to use a diaphragm, just in case, or pills or something."

I was rapidly coming to feel uncomfortable in the guise in which I'd come to the man. But that was like locking the barn after the horse. The same type of help he was offering Lucy.

"All the regrets in the world can't undo what is done," I said. "Will you help us, or will you not."

"You are absolutely right, absolutely." He took his prescription pad and spent several moments writing a couple of lines. He tore the top sheet off, and folded it and extended it halfway toward me.

"You are right, Mr. Keindly. And I am sorry if I have seemed unhelpful. I'll help you, all right. I've written on this page the name of a man who should be able to offer you some assistance. His office may seem a little seamy, and he may come after your daughter with sharpened coat hangers and—" He cut himself off by dropping the paper on the desk in front of me and leaning way back in his chair and laughing.

Loud, vulgar peels of laughter, through which he had to hold the top of his head. He frightened me. But loud noises and *nonsequiturs* usually do.

I picked up his prescription for my problems, and opened it. It read:

> Albert Samson
> Indianapolis, Indiana
> U.S.A. World

132

The bastard knew all along who I was.

There are times in this business when all the words in the world cannot express exactly what has gone on in the shortest period of time.

There was nothing I could do but wait until he had had his laugh. Usually I try to be a good sport, but it is a fairly well-established fact that I do not take big jokes on me all that well. Leander Crystal's last chance of buying me off went up in gales of laughter in Lafayette, Indiana, that afternoon.

By the time he was snuffing to control himself I was looking at his pictures. One was not of him at all, I didn't know who. One looked like a newspaper shot of him receiving a plaque or something from somebody. And the third was of the doctor in his full-dress Army uniform. There was something wrong about that picture. I didn't know what.

Chivian had just cooled down; I was heated up.

"Nice little joke, Doc," I said with my best Bogart voice, and my best Cagney stare.

"Well, I'm sorry, Samson. But I'd been warned you might come around and I've been checking the names and addresses of new patients against the phone book and a Lafayette address register. Mr. Keindly had neither a phone nor an address. I would have let you go on, but I just don't have any more time today to see how a real private eye works." He was smirking, the bastard.

"At this point do you answer questions or do you play cute?"

"It should depend on the questions, I know. But I have to balance the fact that I have nothing in my life to hide against the balls you have coming here to ask me questions at all."

"It depends on how good a friend of Leander Crystal's you are."

"Does this mean that you are accepting his offer?"

"Not necessarily, but you have already answered that question."

"I know." He sighed. "I had hoped for some style from you, Samson, but all I get is two-bit games. Leander and I were in the Army together. We kept in touch, and when he settled in Indianapolis, he invited me to try it too. I did and became his family's doctor. After a while I decided I wanted to open a clinic in the area, he helped me get the loan, we got a good deal here and here I have remained. I go to Indianapolis, usually once every other week, to see Fleur. Then I play golf with Leander in the afternoon. Sometimes I don't stay the afternoons. Is there anything else you want to know? If so, please make it brief. I have patients waiting."

"Nothing else," I said.

I got up and left the room, closing the door quietly behind me.

There were no patients in the waiting room. There was only Mrs. Rogers.

She spoke as I walked by. "Did you give him the good time you had in store for me? He needed it. He's been pretty nervous the last few. . . ."

I didn't hear the end of her solicitude. I had closed the outer door, and at the same time she had stopped talking. I heard the echo of laughter as I went out to my car, but that might just have been my imagination.

I drove like hell to get back to Indianapolis. Combination of mood and circumstances. If Leander Crystal had friends like that, I figured he didn't need enemies. In the first half of the trip I also thought up many other novel notions.

But I was relaxing some by the time I got to the city. It was pushing five, and coming into town during the rush hour going out made me feel better. More reflective. Reflective enough to figure out what had been wrong with that Army picture. Basically nothing. It had not lied at all. It must have been when Chivian was something like thirty years old, what with medical school and all.

Nearly thirty and with a receding hairline. Much more recessed than it was today. I realized why he had had to hold onto his head even during his moment of triumph. The bastard was bald, bald as an egg.

Bald, one might say, as Leander Crystal. The Doublemint twins.

I laughed aloud from Kessler Boulevard all the way to Thirty-eighth Street, no mean distance. And I only stopped then because I was getting tired and a traffic cop looked at me kind of funny.

The rest of the way in I figured out that without the wig and the tan Chivian would look pretty much like Leander. Superficial description anyway. Chivian a little taller, and a little heavier and a little older. And a lot nastier.

Somehow I didn't figure Crystal for the nasties. It was as if Chivian were sort of the poor relation, the pale imitation, the crude Crystal.

And it passed through my mind that they might be more closely related than friends; a notion I decided was worth a little effort. I made a note.

I had no traffic all the way home.

But I had had heavy traffic at home.

The mail was on the floor as usual, and I ground it into the floorboards as I came in. There was something of interest, a letter from the New York Birth Certificates Office.

But other things were not right. My office desk drawers were open. The same at the desk and bureau in my living room. I always close my drawers all the way. It's not something I am careless about in my dotage.

I had had little visitors.

I went to my files. They do not lock. I've never needed a lock.

I opened to *C.* The Crystal file was missing. The folder containing the negatives and the prints so kindly supplied by the officers of the law, as well as my Fishman records and Graham letters.

I was nearly in shock. I ran back to my office desk on which there resided one beautiful, gorgeous, exquisite set of prints of the Crystal office papers, in ten organized piles. My working copy. Sitting on the desk, beautiful and gorgeous, and ready for work. If I needed anything else to get me down to business, this was it. What a ridiculous game—two grown men playing "let's raid each other's office!"

My only salvation was that Crystal had not known that Miller gave me two sets of prints, not one. And I thanked Crystal for his added message: there is something in them. I presumed my visitor was Crystal.

I opened the letter from New York and examined the birth certificate of Eloise Crystal. Delivering physician was Henry Chivian. Surprise, surprise.

That certificate started the new Crystal file, and a picture of it started the new safety file which would remain undeveloped, on film, and hidden. Unless needed.

I sat at my desk and addressed an envelope to Leander Crystal. Into it I tearfully put his check for fifty thousand dollars. I had the passing thought that instead, I should ask him for lots more. What would he do?

But that would be immoral. Of course, if I were bothering about things moral, the proper thing for me to do would be to keep quiet, drop the case and send the man back his money anyway.

If I cashed the check, under any circumstances, I would have felt guilty. Not that one cannot adjust to living with guilt. . . .

I almost put Chivian's prescription in the envelope as well, but thought better of it. It was a sample of the handwriting of the man. Instead I took a picture of it and dropped the original in the file with Eloise's birth certificate. It might be a clue. And Leander wouldn't need it to enjoy the report of my adventure in Lafayette. Probably he was already getting that.

I paused for a thought. The mail was where it should have been when I came in, but the drawers were not. That either meant that my visitor was more careful about putting the mail back where he found it than he had been about the drawers, or that the mail came after my visitor.

Odds on the second one. Mail usually comes about two. Crystal had decided to have the stuff picked up this morning. Before I'd seen Chivian. That was curious. And meant that Chivian had called him, probably the night before, to tell him that a Mr. Keindly was coming, but no one knew where from. And Crystal had decided that this meant that I was not to be "reasoned" with.

There were a lot of presumptions, indeed. It was possible that it was not Crystal who had taken the Crystal file. But I had a hard time coming up with an alternative. Except maybe Eloise. But why?

Ugh. Too much. I gathered the remaining set of my precious photos, and went sleuthily downstairs, and to my neighborhood drugstore. There I bought up all the rolls of black-and-white 35 mm film he had, along with some potato chips and a Table Talk rhubarb and apple pie. I returned to the office.

I started my evening by taking pictures of all the pictures I was lucky still to have. When I had finished popping pics, I hid the undeveloped films under my mattress and started to work seriously on the Crystal records.

30

I would not have believed how much unintelligible information can be packed onto 1,241 pictures. It took me till past eleven to realize that financial records are not my strong point. I mean, I knew it all along, but it took a long time to realize that meant I should start elsewhere. As with my doctor pictures, it might well be most efficient to leave them to an expert.

Conduct an audit, what a fetching idea. Only I didn't know anyone who could do it. So I called Maude. Maude knows people who will do anything.

"Berrrtie! How the hell are you? I was just this moment picking up the phone to give you a ring. You know, shoot the breeze a little." When she is tired that is her notion of a fabulous lie. Maude virtually never talks anything but business.

"I need a name, Maude, someone to go over a lot of financial records and tell me what they mean."

She thought for a moment and said, "I presume since you are calling me you want a person who can keep his mouth shut."

"Very shut."

"Very? Is there likely to be some heat on him?"

"I don't know how likely. But I'm beginning to think anything is possible. I have some records, you see, and I would very much prefer that nobody knew I had them."

"Well," she said, "I have a man who does a lot of things for me, but he is probably pretty high for you."

"How high?"

"Like fifty to get in the door."

"Will he do it on a contingency basis? Say, a hundred, plus more if he gets hustled? I don't really think he will be."

"He'll do it."

"Done."

"Name is Andrew Elmitt, 4552 Park Avenue. Phone is, let me see, Humbolt 6-9292. Send your phone number with the stuff. Special delivery if you want it done fast. He'll call you a day or two after he gets it."

"I don't want anybody getting blackmailed if there turns out to be anything there."

"Your mind is too florid, Berrrrtie. Elmitt is completely reliable, and besides I've got enough on him to get him into prison and tax manipulator's heaven."

"Fair enough. Now all I have to worry about is you."

"A good point there. I'll call the gentleman to check, and tell him to expect a package tomorrow. If I don't call you back in ten minutes, it's on."

I spent the ten minutes trying to figure out how likely Maude was to try to blackmail someone. But I guessed that it wasn't really likely. At least 4 to 1 against.

After another five I decided to call Miller. No more sitting around on my butt trying to figure the most delicate way to do things. I was for action now.

Miller sounded tired and bored. Poor man, I try to bring a little spice into his life but he doesn't always appreciate it.

"So, you're really stuck on going ahead, are you?"

"Yeah. You got that name right? Chivian, Henry, MD." I spelled it for him, even the MD. That's what I mean about the spice. It isn't everybody who'd do that for a friend.

"All right, all right. But what I want to know is what I get out of this."

"You get the first police information about any illegal doings. You get it all."

"Is that before or after you sell the story to the papers?"

"What do you care, if you get that big bust that propels you into the lieutenancy you desire? By the way, I have something else that might interest you."

"Oh." He didn't sound interested.

"Somebody came in and stole the lovely pictures you had made for me."

"Oh, yeah? They get both sets?" He still didn't sound interested.

"No. I was lucky. They were looking for one set and the negatives, and that's what they got, plus all my other records."

"Well, as it happens I had a set made for myself. If you accidentally burn up the ones you have left you can borrow mine." So that's why he wasn't interested. He had already been interested enough in my case to

138

keep copies of everything. Army files; police records. Very nice. What a nice gentleman.

He continued. "Anything else? I haven't got time to fuck around with you on the phone."

"I know," I said. "You've gotta get home to the wife."

For some reason he hung up on me.

It's like with food. There are just some people who can take spice and some who cannot.

I had asked him to get me Army records on Chivian and when he found out where he lived before the Army, police records. Maybe Ames, Iowa?

I gathered the financial piles from my Crystal collection and put them in a small envelope. Then I put the small envelope in a larger one and addressed it to Andrew Elmitt. I covered it with stamps, wrote "Special Delivery" on it with a blood-colored crayon from my animal-drawing set, and went out and mailed it.

31

But I couldn't sleep. It had been quite a day. If I'd been in a passive mood I would have been depressed. As it was I watched the cracks in the ceiling, to see if they were going to move. I studied them for faces, and then for animals. I heard voices in the office. I heard voices in the hall. I saw Chivian laughing at me. And I saw those chicken pox scars and wondered how many kids she had.

It occurred to me that it was very strange that Leander Crystal had bought the house Mrs. Forebush now lived in over a year before she needed it. Especially with Estes alive. Also that he had refitted it in such detail, down to locks on the doors. If he had bought it in anticipation of Mrs. Forebush needing it, why those particular fittings. Why seclusive shrubs? And why twin beds?

Why indeed. Especially if he had been doing it to rent the house. To an alien who did not register in January of—what year?

I got out of bed and consulted my notes. In January of 1955, 1956, 1957, 1958, and 1959. I returned to bed.

Presumably in 1954 she either registered or entered the country giving

413 East Fiftieth Street as her address. Her last address known to the Immigration Department.

So it had to be. That after Leander bought the house, he rented it to this unknown alien. With twin beds, yet.

This I found of considerable interest. This is not how fortunes of two million dollars are built back up to ten million. So clearly the goal of operation was not profit. In the same period of time he had found money to pay to Jacques Chaulet and to Chivian. So why? A decent question. If not for money, then what for, love?

Hmmmmm. An indecent question.

I got out of bed again and called Miller.

But the off chance that he was still at the station was off. I considered for a moment calling him at home, but not even I would do that. And besides he couldn't help me at home. I wanted him to get information from the Immigration Department, or would it be Justice Department now, about this alien, unnamed. It would keep though. Until tomorrow. What's another day?

I had more trouble keeping until tomorrow. I was excited. I found a lot of animals in the cracks before I got to sleep.

32

"I'm sorry to bother you, but I am from the U.S. Department of Immigration, and I'd like a few moments of your time."

Up close the old guy looked about sixty-five, lots of white hair and in pretty good shape. It's the thin ones who last a long time.

"My name is Joe Jenkins. I'm eighty-three years old, youngster, never had a drop to drink in my life, I've never had no trouble with any kind of police, and I've never worried a day in my life. Now is there anything else you want to know?"

It was a little after nine thirty. I'd been out a half hour canvassing Mrs. Forebush's neighbors looking for people who'd been around since 1953 or so. I was trying to get a little information about the alien tenant. It had occurred to me that somebody in the neighborhood might remember her. It seemed worth a shot.

The way the Forebush house is placed, there are a lot of neighbors who might be able to keep track of a tenant there. It is one house in from a corner house, and the other side borders on an alley. That gave me the corner house and two or three around the corner whose backyards might overlook Forebush's, as well as the house across the alley which gave me two families because it was a double. And maybe a few across the street.

I had worked my way around the corner and although I had found a lot of people who lived in the area that long, or longer, only one remembered anything at all. She was a lady named Fay. She had raised her children, twins, Newton and Norman, in her house and she intended to die there, or so she said. At length. She remembered vaguely that there had been a young couple in the house "before the Forebush woman got it." She didn't know really anything about them, she only saw the man a few times. It was possible that Newton or Norman remembered more. They were married now. She gave me their names and addresses.

It was the best I had done.

I had stopped at the two houses which faced Forebush's across the street, but found only one occupied. A girl, about twenty, was unpacking crates and had just moved in. I asked about the former residents, hoping to track them down. The question didn't turn her on. They had died in a car crash the month before.

I was now at the double on the same side as Forebush's but across the alley. My last chance. The old guy I'd seen on the porch the first time I'd visited Fiftieth Street.

I asked him how long he had lived in the neighborhood.

"Lived? Here? Since creation, sonny, since creation. I've been here as long as it has, since 1926. I bought it outright then, and a good thing I did because it was a lifesaver during the depression, a real lifesaver."

He seemed willing to chat.

"Now, what do you want? I can tell you anything you want to know. For instance, the house you just came from. The old geezer piled them up on the highway to Kokomo last month, on the twenty-sixth it was. He was too old to drive. Too old. Even had his license taken away for six months about four years back. But he got it back. Now see what it's

141

got him. And his little woman. She deserved better, she did. Real nice little lady.

"And the house you went to before that—"

I cut him off, fascinated though I was. "It's the one next door." I pointed across the alley.

"I reckoned it was," he said sagely. "At least you've been in and out of it a few times the last couple of weeks. What is it? Mrs. Forebush figuring to sell it? Nice little house, you could do worse."

"No, I'm just trying to find out about the people who lived there before Mrs. Forebush."

"Ah, that's right. Some government official or something you said. What's the matter? They do something? Are they wanted?"

"No, I just need to know about them."

"Well, let's see." He scratched his chin. He really did. "For a long time there it belonged to Railroad Mackeson. Would it be him that you were wanting to know about?"

"I don't know. Was he the occupant of the house just before Mrs. Forebush?"

"Well, the only one that was worth a damn. But he's dead now. That ain't gonna help you."

"Who came into the house after him?" The serial approach.

"Well, lemme see. House stood empty for a while while the kids wrangled over who got it. Then they decided to sell it and split the money instead. That would be 1952 or 1953. Just about the time Ike was getting himself elected. For the first time, that was. Good time to sell a house. So they sold it, pretty quick too. I remember that the new owner, whoever it was, had some changes done. Bit of a shame too, not that old Mackeson ever did much with the garden, but the yard looks a whole lot bigger with flowers than it did with big bushes. I guess that's why it stood empty for so long."

"It stood empty?"

"Yes, sir. Several months. The way I figure the owner bought it to rent out. Had it fixed up like. I saw a lot of furniture go in. And then I figure he couldn't rent it for quite a while. Maybe a bad time for renting houses furnished. I don't know. But there it stood."

"Then what happened?"

"Well, except for a young couple lived there for a few months, it's been Mrs. Forebush."

142

"I think it's the young couple that I want to know about."

He peered at me. He wore no glasses. "Why? Why them? Is it because the lady was a foreigner?"

"That's it, old-timer."

"Where'd you say you was from?"

"Department of Immigration."

"Why'd you come here then?"

"We can't find her. That house is the last address we have for her."

"Well, by God! She ain't lived there for more'n fifteen years. Why you just getting around to her now?"

"You know how it is. We get a lot of paperwork and things pile up."

"Whewee! Son, let me tell you a little something. That's no way to run a business. I run a couple of mighty successful businesses in my time, and this one of yours ain't gonna last that way."

"What do you know about the young couple?"

"Not much. They wasn't here very long. Spent a lot of time in the house, I can tell you that. Both of them. They'd go shopping together. Didn't seem to get along all that well. You can tell about couples. I guess'd they were just married before they came here, and I could see after a while why there was some troubles. She started putting a belly on her, and I don't mean from overeating. Now my wife, God rest her soul, she could have told you how old it was to within a couple of weeks. But I don't remember."

"Did they have the child before they left?"

"Nope. I just figure they got fed up of the place or maybe each other. They just left one day, with some suitcases. Didn't come back."

"Can you tell me what they looked like?"

"Well, they'll have changed a lot by now, of course. But at the time." He thought. "The girl, apart from her belly, a little slip of a thing. Brown hair, pretty, young. Maybe twenty, twenty-five. He was a lot older. Well, maybe not a lot older, but he looked it. Like forty or so. He had brown hair too, well as I could remember. What there was of it."

"He was bald?"

"Pert near. Reckon he's looking pretty shiny by now."

"Do you remember when they left?"

"Not really. But Mrs. Forebush'll tell you. She didn't move in but a couple of weeks after. Real nice little lady, that Mrs. Forebush. Real

143

friendly. And real cute little package for her age. You reckon she'd be interested in an older man? Older, but young at heart? You ask her that for me, will you, youngster?"

"Mr. Jenkins, I would, but I somehow figure that in the fifteen years you've been here you might have had a chance to ask her yourself."

"Sonny, I might have done but that wouldn't be quite right, would it? I mean with one wife already. My Mrs., God rest her soul, she only died four months ago. I reckoned to have a little chat with Mrs. Forebush, but I can't hardly do that before decent mourning is over, now, can I? I just thought, you know, if you're friendly with her that you could sound her out for me. That wouldn't be immoral, now, would it? And then I'd have a little more to go on, a little more to look forward to in the next eight months."

"Tell you what I'll do. If I can fit it into the conversation I'll ask her how she feels about remarriage. And if she'd consider it, I'll give you thumbs up as I leave, how's that?"

"That'll do real well, sonny. Anymore it seems like no one will do a favor for an old man. I really appreciate it. I purely do. Mighty fetching little piece she is. For her age."

I left him drooling mentally, and with each step toward Mrs. Forebush's door I felt more and more like a Golden Years Pandarus.

Mrs. Forebush was in, and surprised to see me so early. Earlier than she usually took visitors, but I imposed. After all we had a relationship. I only stayed a few minutes and told her what I was working on. She couldn't add much, just that she had moved in September 14, 1954, and that when she had moved in the previous tenants had left a lot of stuff. Not a lot of stuff to live with, but a lot of stuff to have left. Beds, one each in two of the rooms, some furniture, food, pots and pans, dishes, silverware, sheets and bedding.

It sounded very much like the stuff Leander had put in after he bought the house.

"What did you do with it?" I asked her.

"Put the whole lot out. All to the Salvation Army. Mr. Crystal told me before he left that when I moved in I could do absolutely whatever I wanted to with it, that it was mine. And that's what I wanted."

"And was it only the girl the Immigration people asked you about?"

144

"Yes."

"I've been talking with your neighbor across the alley."

"The old man. Sits in the front window all day keeping track of everything that goes on in this street."

"His wife died recently."

"I know. I didn't know her but it was probably the effort of cleaning all his field glasses and sharpening his pencils."

I took my leave.

Walking down the steps to my car I gave the old man thumbs up.

At the car door I paused and then I walked back over to have a couple more words with him.

"She really likes me, huh?" His expression was as close to a leer as he could manage with no teeth.

"I didn't say that. I just asked her if she had ever considered remarrying, and she said that she had."

"Oh, boy," he said.

"I wanted to ask you something else. You don't by any chance keep any records of goings-on down this street, do you? Like of cars that come down here and so on."

"Don't I! You just wait there, sonny."

I waited, not believing, half hoping. It would be a bit sticky tracking down lists of cars registered fifteen years before, but I could have it done. Money is a wonderful lubricant.

He brought out an old ledger and showed me the first page.

"I started in 1935. I had figured out there was gonna be a war. I thought somebody might be interested in just who came and went around here. Could be useful. You know, if there was somebody on every street, keeping track of comings and goings. Maybe catch us a spy or two."

"Could I see a little farther on?"

"Say when, sonny."

He thumbed on slowly. About three-quarters through, he came to a blank page. "That's it."

"There's no more?" The last page was titled "December 21 to December 31, 1949."

"What do you want, sonny? War was long over by then. And my eyes aren't what they used to be. Any help to you?"

145

" 'Fraid not. But I appreciate it. I purely do."

"Oh, that's OK. Never did figure it was worth much to anybody. Would take a whole network of people like me."

"I guess it would. Take it easy."

"Say, sonny, what with times gettin' permissive, do you think that six months' mourning would be enough?"

"Still a year. Good people still respect traditions."

"I guess so. Guess so." I left him scratching his chin.

33

It was half past eleven. I had lunch and I spent the bulk of the remaining office hours serving papers. I was doing it very cunningly. Very efficiently. I was nearly halfway done with a four-day job in less than two days. I really regretted taking the job, but what's a fellow to do?

At four thirty I was on the east side, a little past the Fair Grounds on Thirty-eighth Street. I called Miller. And found him in, as usual. But cheery.

"I've got a case, Al. A decent real case. Extortion. I guess somebody had too many to keep for himself and decided to let poor old Miller have a crack. I'll be out of the office for a while anyway. Most of the time. You were lucky to catch me in."

"You won't need me to confess to trespassing then, good."

"This might be a break. What can I do for you? I have some records here. Army, hometown police, Lafayette police, and medical association. I'll leave them for you."

"Thanks, but before you go, could you do me one more? I'm looking for a lost alien. Could you ask the Department of Immigration what they have on a young female alien, I don't know the name, but who lived here at 413 East Fiftieth Street from the spring of 1954 to maybe September of 1954. The address is the last one known for her. They sent a man asking for her for five straight years after '54."

"That'll be the Justice Department, Al. Not Immigration." He paused. "This is the same case, is it?"

"Yeah, it's the same case. What's the matter? You getting a little

146

touchy about handing out your favors now that you are a big lieutenant?"

"I'm not lieutenant yet, Al."

"As I am only too aware. Get the stuff for me, will you, Sergeant?"

"Oh, hell. Sure."

"And make it snappy. I wouldn't want to have to put in a bad word with your captain."

He laughed. "My captain, huh? Gartland wouldn't understand you if you did talk to him. You talk good English."

I said, "Good luck." And I hung up.

Being out east, it seemed a waste to drive straight home just to go get the Chivian files from police headquarters. But I couldn't think of anything else to do. I compromised and stopped at a store for some unshelled walnuts. Then I drove home enjoying for the second straight day the drive against the general flow of rush-hour traffic. I split the difference, and parked halfway between police headquarters and Samson headquarters.

With a pocketful of walnuts I headed for the cops. But all my plans were in vain. Numb Nuts was nowhere to be seen. My gift stayed in my pocket. I picked up the files and headed home.

On the street I cracked a couple in my hand, and picked out the nutmeats. It's not hard to do them in your hand, but after a few your hand begins to hurt. Why bother? I left the rest for later, maybe to scatter across the floor to surprise a burglar in case I had night visitors or something. Or to save. I'm not all that keen on walnuts. I had more gentle work to save my hands for. Turning pages. And pages and pages.

Which I did all evening. Not even a call from my woman dissuaded me. My loving woman.

Man, that's dedication.

It was files night at Samson's.

First Chivian's Army record. It located his birth in New York City in 1915. A war baby. He had been drafted as a doctor in 1943. He had served in the same outfit as Leander Crystal and Joshua Graham. The only notation of interest was that he had "appeared as a witness at the inquest following the death of Private Joshua Graham."

He had no New York police record. And no record in Lafayette. No unusual information from the medical association, in which he was a member in good standing.

At least I got his home address. And the information that he was not married when he joined the Lafayette AMA. No indication if he ever had been. He joined in 1957. The year he told me he moved to Lafayette.

Not exactly a pile of information. But I was not daunted. I went on to the nonfinancial piles of Leander Crystal.

In a move of infinite craft, I decided to hit the piles in the order I figured would be easiest to understand.

I started with the money. I had pictures of several of the bills. Enough to see they were most likely in sequence. Hence new. With my magnifier I estimated the number of edges. I made it about seven and a half thousand bucks, if they were all twenties.

Then I hit the pornography. Not that I expected a great deal from it, but I had decided to go with what was easiest to understand. Which didn't turn out to be quite that. I mean I'm not that sure that I understand pornography.

But I did notice one thing. Although I had only taken pictures of half the stuff—and it lost a lot in the transition from color to black and white—it was clear that not all of it was professional. Some was, but other pictures were just snapshots of naked ladies. Enlarged to the same size as the others, but just pictures. Almost portraits, if the enlarger had been a little more scrupulous about getting the whole head on each print.

The personnel varied. Except for one of whom there was a series of pictures. Profiles. A rather frail lady, with an increasingly protuberant midsection.

I could almost feel the camera being held by a balding man of about forty, give or take a few years. My only problem was figuring out which of the available balding men of that age was squeezing the shutter.

And figuring out just what else he had been squeezing.

I let it go, thinking only of how willing my lecherous old gentleman would be to identify one of these pictures.

OK, granted it *was* my missing alien tenant.

Could Leander have been the gentleman of the house? I mean *could* he have been? Was it possible? What about his other family? Or was I left with Chivian?

Or with someone else.

And then I thought about the high shrubs and electric garage door device Leander had put in. I had nasty thoughts about two bald men and a frail pregnant foreign lady.

It was worth a break. I had some dinner.

When I moved back across the room after a quick pair of sandwiches I decided to let the wicked rest. I took instead the photographs from Crystal's scrapbook. I used to keep a scrapbook. I figured it might not be too hard to understand.

A slight underestimation. Mementos are fine, if you know just what they mement. I spent about an hour going through pages and pages of the early entries: ticket stubs, programs, paper clippings, official letters, less official notes in French, and pictures. All more or less from the wartime, maybe a little before and a little after. The only general notion I got was that the man had been a fairly fast liver. The notes in French were sweet.

There were no references to anybody that I recognized, apart from Eisenhower and Churchill.

The war had been an active, exciting, expanding time for my juvenile delinquent from Ames, Iowa. But it didn't help me much.

The later entries made more sense. He had clippings that I had seen in the *Star*, for instance. Plus a couple I hadn't seen from the *News*, the *Star*'s afternoon brother. Only on rereading about the marriage did I realize how much older than Fleur Graham Leander Crystal was. When he first came to Indianapolis in 1946 to go to Butler's Business College he was twenty-six years old. Fleur was sixteen. He had been halfway around the world, had seen all there was to see in a war, and from the clippings and letters, he had not limited himself to the bullets and strategy aspects.

She had seen nothing. Was, from the accounts I had, a relatively quiet, relatively awkward little girl.

Enter Leander.

A love match.

The phone rang. I picked it up and expected the party himself.

"Mr. Samson? This is your tax man." The words were spaced to emphasize their meaning. "I received today a parcel from you. I wondered if you could give me some rather more specific instructions

149

about its contents. There is a great deal here, you understand, and if I know what I am looking for it will help me approach things."

"I understand your problem, but there isn't a lot that I can do to help you."

"Perhaps if I am a little more specific. Can you tell me if we are looking for tax fraud, or evidence of fiscal mismanagement, or money going to mysterious places which might be evidence of support of a mistress, or what?"

"I need to have some indication, first, of what each entry is. No need to make detailed counts of money spent yet. I don't know quite what I am looking for, but the first step is the identification of each entry. If it will help any, I am most interested in the period of time around 1953 and 1954."

"All right, I'll try to identify that time and work on it first. Perhaps, if you could, you will come by tomorrow. Say early afternoon. By then I shall have gone through matters once and perhaps we will be able to define the problem more specifically."

"All right."

"You will take precautions, if you believe them necessary, to make sure you are not followed. I understand that there is some danger."

"I'm not absolutely sure of that, but I shall take precautions."

"Good. Good night."

Good, maybe getting better. The tempo of life seemed to be picking up. I was excited again. Still.

Excited enough to face, again, piles of pictures. From the scrapbook I got a little more. A few things having to do with young Eloise. And then the pages sort of thinned out. I got the idea that the book itself was a relic of a more exciting, perhaps less mature period for the man.

I went on. Pictures of miscellaneous papers. Junk mail: most of the loose papers in his desk drawer had been very miscellaneous indeed. I found nothing in it.

I came to his address book. Which turned out to be women. Forty-two of them. Which gave me something to think about. There is no telling when they dated from, but that was not an evil number over fifteen years.

The many secrets of a man. I didn't know what to do with so many secrets.

But it occurred to me that the number itself told me something. That they were all or mostly professional. No man in Crystal's financial position could have that many free girlfriends without having paid at least the price of gossip. And any gossip would have gotten back to Maude. But Maude had given Crystal a clean gossip record. Q.E.D.

I recalled the clothes in his office. An orderly man—not prone to scandal. And willing to go to some expense to avoid it. And trouble too. I wondered if he wore his Secret Office Wig when visiting his Secret Ladies. It sounded like surprises from cereal boxes.

I decided to call Miller.

He was there, but the stuff I wanted wasn't.

"Look, Al, they're only human, even at the Justice Department. If you had the name I might have had it, but the earliest it will be in is tomorrow. Give it a rest, will you? I only sent it out this afternoon."

He was right, of course. I had forgotten that it was only that afternoon that I had asked him for the information on my missing alien.

A bad sign. A bad sign. Losing track of time. I put my stuff away and headed toward the bed, by way of a sleeping pill. I don't take them often, so when I do—Boom!

34

I woke up low and impatient. I had my tax man to see. I didn't want to wait until the afternoon for something Crystalish to do. But there was nothing. Tax man in the afternoon, phone call to Miller in the evening. But what in the morning?

A leisurely breakfast.

Serving papers.

At one forty-five, I pulled up in front of 4552 North Park Avenue. Not Park Avenue in New York, but a rather classy, big Georgian house, with pillars. I didn't know if I could afford it. In fact I knew I couldn't afford it.

I rang the bell. A man about 6 feet 6 and very thin opened the door and waved me in. "I've been expecting you, Mr. Samson. Very interesting documents you've left me with." He led me down the hall across the width of a long living room to a sun porch, which was next to a screened porch. I've served papers on people in houses like these but I've never hired one before. I am a better employee than employer. And perhaps best neither.

But the guy, for all his heights, was understanding of us little fellows. "You are not quite comfortable here, Mr. Samson? Don't worry, you don't have to pay for it. I inherited the house and some money to keep it up. I do work like yours for my health. Sit down." He proffered a deep wicker chair next to a low round wicker table which was covered with yellow lined paper and my photographs.

"I'm Andrew Elmitt." We strained, from the depths of our chairs, to shake hands.

"I can see why you were not able to give me a good idea of what is going on here. Primarily because there is a good deal going on. Though I am surprised that you are most interested in the period you mentioned."

"Why?" I said, my first nongrunted utterance.

"Why, because it is precisely before about 1956 that there is absolutely nothing going on. Oh, a little, but there is so much less money to be played with then. It's all the little gettings and spendings. A few things which seem out of place, like these checks to a man called Chaulet, but otherwise fairly routine." He dragged out the word "fairly" as if he were a lawyer and didn't want to be held to it.

"But since 1956, beautiful. Whoever owns the original records inherited a lot of money, I take it. And he was not altogether used to handling it, I take it. But the man has a gift. Caution and daring. It's really a beautiful story. I mean"—he paused, once again aware of my presence—"beautiful in money terms. Financial world stuff. You know."

I knew. I also knew that Maude had got me just the kind of man I needed, much more of the world of money than the world of the people who had the money.

"OK," I said, "give me a rundown. You can start after he got his cash and we'll work backwards."

"A rundown," he said. "Well, it's a little hard to put in terms a layman can understand. . . ."

He wasn't kidding. It was about an hour before I felt that I had the gist. Leander inherited money. Leander wasn't used to having big money. Leander learned about having big money. Leander made the big money grow bigger, very cleverly, and after a while very fast. Leander had guts. Leander had guts worth about ten or twelve million, before the 1970 recession.

Leander was a poor boy with latent talent he had been lucky enough to get a chance to develop. Lucky enough? Or made his own luck. It interested me that the man who emphasized to me that Fleur should not have to suffer from not having enough money to indulge her hypochondria had taken chances that at some times could have ruined them, had they soured.

But of course they had flowered, and everyone was in clover. Especially Leander.

"And," said Elmitt with a *coup de grâce* kind of tone, "there is the little matter of his Swiss bank account."

"What?"

"Ah." He laughed. "I thought that might get your interest."

"Mr. Elmitt," I said, "I am interested in everything you have to say. It's just that I have more than a little difficulty understanding it. Maybe I should take a course."

"Maybe you should, maybe you should. The study of finance can be a fascinating hobby, or business, as the case may be."

"The Swiss thing?"

"Yes. Now I can't guarantee it, but this page and this page"—he waved, economically, two pages—"have the distinct smell of a Swiss bank account."

"How distinct?"

"Oh, pretty distinct. It seems to have about a million and a quarter in it, and it is identified only by a number." It was the straightest sentence I had gotten out of him. I wondered if he was tiring.

"I can't be certain, of course, but they usually imply a certain amount of tax fraud. Would that be of any use to you?"

"I think it would," I said.

"Oh, good," he said, and started gathering papers. I stopped him.

"There are a couple of things we have yet to settle, Mr. Elmitt. The other material. And I'm not sure that I can afford your going on with these."

"Well, what are we set at so far?"

"A hundred," I said. As if it were thousands.

"Up it to a hundred and a half and I'll give you the works on this stuff."

"OK," I said, "Consider it upped."

"Good. I said you wouldn't have to pay to support this place. But you can help my daughter to get a new dress. I would have hated to be teased and then not be given the chance to run through all the calculations." There was a large adding machine on a desk in the corner of the room. I mean, what was a sun-room supposed to be for? Why not add in the sun?

"About the years before 1956?"

He sighed, and waved at two small piles. "Outcome," he said as he patted the first pile. "Income," and he patted the next, a couple of sheets. "It doesn't take a genius to figure them out."

I let it go at that. I wasn't a genius. I put one pile in each of my jacket pockets, and let him show me his toys on the way out. He even had a little computer in the basement. But I didn't rue my investment, or incipient investment, because he also had a pinball machine sitting right next to the computer. "For my son," he said when he saw me looking at it, and smiling.

I bet. I would almost have bet that he didn't even have a son. But after his hundred and fifty, I didn't have much betting money left.

I shoved off and agreed to wait for his call.

35

As I walked down the hall toward my office I realized that my door was open. Wide open, not just ajar.

My heart started to pound. I hate surprises, especially when I know one is coming but don't know what, or in this case, who it is. Whether to man my defenses, or trot out my sweets.

I considered just heading back out, going over to cop center and talking to Miller there. Reluctantly I decided not to. I didn't want to put the extra pressure of a personal appearance on Miller after the night's foolish call.

But I couldn't go straight into the office.

So I paid a call to my neighborly vacancy next door. I tripped the lock, and skipped in. It is a pair of dirty empty rooms, except for the improvements I have made in the neighborhood of the bathtub. I picked the least growth-ridden corner and put my notebook down in it. Then the set of Crystal photos I'd been carrying around in a manila envelope. Then my jacket with its pockets of in and outcomes.

I wondered, for the several steps back to the firetrap I call home, just who or what was waiting for me.

When I peeked around the edge of the open doorway, I began to suspect a what. My office was empty.

After making one quick move to see if anyone was behind the door, I went in as quietly as I could. I tiptoed to my living-room door. It too was open. Before looking in I stopped to listen. I heard nothing. Maybe I had just left it all open as I went out in the morning. Though I try to be careful about such things, it could happen. I framed a mental picture of myself tippy-toeing around my own empty living quarters. A shadower afraid of his own shadow.

But how does a man live if he doesn't take himself seriously?

I tiptoed to my back room.

My dining-room chair was turned around, facing my window. On one of its broad elm arms I saw a slouched walnut-colored head.

It didn't move. I stood there for what seemed like an eternity, and it didn't move.

I glanced around the room. No other people, otherwise apparently unchanged. I looked back at the back of my former client's head.

I didn't have the faintest idea of what to do.

I went to her, still tiptoeing. I looked at her face. Eyes closed, pale. Unmoving.

I took her hand. It was warm.

She opened her eyes and looked into mine. Leaving her hand in mine she stretched slowly. And slowly woke up.

"I've been waiting quite awhile," she said. The sleep left a fuzz on her ordinarily sleek speech. I let go her hand and rocked back gently and sat on the floor in front of her. Inadvertently it left me looking up her skirt. That made me uncomfortable, so I got up and sat on the windowsill instead. From there I got preoccupied with the low cut of her dress. She was sporting a fair share of teen-age cleavage.

That made me uncomfortable too. I went and got my telephone chair and pulled it up in front of her. Neither above nor below. The third time was a charm. My attention fixed on her baggy eyes and her pallidness.

She sat up. "I wanted to know what you are doing. And why," she said.

"I can see you've been going through a hard time. Problems at home?"

"Yes," she said, "Ever since you started messing around." She fell silent, as we both pondered the fact that it had been she who originally started my messing around.

"I want you to stop," she said with an air of finality.

"Stop what?" I said. And she started to cry. She continued to cry.

I'm sure it was sincere and all that. But I am not one of those whose hearts of stone are cracked by tears. If she had been in my family I would have told her to shut up or go cry in the hall. Being as she was a guest of sorts, I just let her go on, since it wasn't loud enough to disturb the neighbors. Not that they disturb in this cruddy building. Not that I have any neighbors. One of the things I might have done with that fifty thou would have been to lease myself a foothold in a "nicer" joint.

While she cried it out I made us a pot of tea.

The making lasted just long enough. I poured a mug of tea for myself and a cup for her. I put her cup on a little tray, put a little glass of milk, a box of sugar, and a spoon alongside it on the tray, and put it on the arm of the chair. It was just the right amount of time. I know, because she snuffled a "Thank you." If I'd got it to her much earlier she wouldn't have said anything and might have knocked the tray off with her twistings and agonies.

Maybe not though. It's a pretty big arm on the chair and trays sit firmly.

I sat down again on my telephone chair.

She studied the tea, and then with a little sigh she poured some sugar from the box into the spoon. Two spoonfuls, then milk. I take milk; I can't stand sugar in hot tea. But each to his own. She also spilled some sugar on the tray which she would have avoided if she had poured the sugar into the spoon over the cup. Not a child of tidy habits. Men who live alone get picky that way. I can't go on much longer living alone. It's eroding what is left of my charming and delicate personality.

She stirred her tea and the social action made her into a woman-girl

156

again. As such she tried a gambit. "I thought that once you liked me." She looked up at me with big wet brown eyes. The crying had brought color to her face. She didn't look half bad, but I could hardly keep from laughing. When I am really in the middle of some business, and excited about it, I am one coldhearted bastard.

"I did. I do. You were a good boss."

She played it to the hilt, turned away, snuffled, the works. "I didn't mean like that."

"I know," I said. But though I never kick animals, I am not always nice to children. "You want me to stop. What do you want me to stop?"

"Whatever you're doing."

"Are you having a hard time at home?"

"I don't know what is going on, but everybody is just horrible. Mummy has had all kinds of fits and her doctor says she has to stay in and that he will be coming down from Lafayette to see her every couple of days. And Daddy just doesn't know what to do."

"And you think that it is all your fault because you put me on this thing."

"That day that you came over and talked to him I thought it was all over. And all better. I mean Daddy talked to me that day, for the first time like I wasn't a little girl. And he *said* it was going to be all better, and that he was really going to look after Mummy, and everything. And after all, you did find out what I wanted you to find. I just don't understand why you keep on messing around."

And I would have been hard put to tell her. I didn't want to monkey prematurely with the story she had been told. Before I had a complete story to replace it with. But she pressed me.

"Why are you doing it?" she asked.

"I don't like being lied to," I said.

"Who lied to you?" she said sharply.

"I didn't say someone did."

"Who lied to you?"

"I'm not sure."

"Not my father! He didn't lie to you." I noted that she had gotten her problems of terminology straightened out with respect to Leander Crystal.

She was getting on my nerves. "I didn't say anybody had lied to me, I

157

said I don't like being lied to, and that means that when I am told a story I will check it out to make sure that I am not being lied to, and that's what I am doing, and that's what I shall continue to do. And besides," I added, because I felt bloody self-priggy-righteous, "I don't like my office being broken into."

"Who broke into your office?"

I sighed, but spoke carefully. "Somebody interested only in a file marked 'Crystal.' Who do you think it was?"

She was clearly startled. "And that's when you sent the check back?"

Why complicate matters; it was technically the truth even though I had made the resolution beforehand. "That's when I sent the check back," I said.

"And you think he did it?"

I felt out of place as a teacher in elementary detectiveness. "I figured that it was Santa Claus because he forgot the address of your chimney."

"You don't have to be snotty about it."

"I know. I'm just tired."

"I must bore you," she said with a burst of feeling, "something awful."

I just can't understand how it is that older men get mixed up with teen-age girls. They're so damn unreliable. Unless maybe it's because they *are* changeable, and not the same, day after day, minute after minute. But she was wearing me out.

"Don't worry about it, little lady," I said with as much kindness as I could muster. "I am sorry if I am making waves in the Crystal home, but at this point it is certainly not your fault. Blame it on me. I am certainly perverse about such matters, if you know the word. It's why I'm not rich." How true! "I will try to make it as painless as I can. Try to trust me if you can. And if you can't, then I just hope you realize that there is nothing you can do about it."

"Nothing?" she said. I knew what she was thinking. I thought I knew what she was thinking.

"Absolutely nothing."

"OK," she said. She got up and turned for the door and then turned back. "I feel better. I don't know why, but I feel a lot better." I nodded beneficently. At the door she turned again and said, "Thanks for the tea. It was good." She left.

I felt better too. I knew why. Not virtue rewarded, but the fact that no matter how it was settled, I liked this as a last meeting much better than the tense bitter little girl I had talked to at the Crystal house. I had disliked her enough then that I had virtually forgotten about her altogether. Though I wished I had told her to keep her trap shut when she got home, I had a more sympathetic taste in my mouth for my little lady client. Former client.

36

I waited awhile before I called Miller. To segment the parts of my life. Break it all down into more handleable pieces. I had another mug of tea.

I called Miller. That is, I called Police HQ and asked for Miller. Not there, but he had left the stuff for me. "Are you Mr. Samson? Sergeant Miller left an envelope for you. When would you care to pick it up?" I cared to pick it up immediately. I knew the desk man wasn't Numbie. I could tell by the grammar. I was beginning to wonder what had happened to poor old Numb Nuts. I still don't know. I guess I'll have to remember to ask Miller sometime.

I picked up the folder from a clean-cut young cop who was filling in on the desk. I walked home, and on the way in I picked up the items I'd stashed next door.

I had a choice. Leander's tiddly bills or the Immigration file.

I went for the Immigration file.

Annie Lombard; French, unmarried, aged nineteen at time of entry into the United States on April 17, 1954. Admitted as resident alien. Fingerprints enclosed. Address in United States.: 413 East Fiftieth Street, Indianapolis, Indiana. American Consulate in Marseilles stated she had proof of assets of over nine thousand dollars and that her fiancé, an American, had written a letter "guaranteeing" that she would not become a "ward of the state."

In April, 1955, was the first notation that there was no record of an Annie Lombard having registered at a post office, or having left the country.

At that point Immigration had turned the case over to the Justice

159

Department. They had found that she no longer resided at the address given and that persons currently residing at that address knew nothing about her.

There was a covering note stating the presumption that either she had left the country and her leaving had been missed clerically, or that she remained illegally. It also asked for any further information on this "missing alien" which the Indianapolis Police might have.

Altogether a fascinating document. Quite, quite fascinating, considering the information it gave as stacked up against the information I had.

There had never been "friends" at the address given. Only a bald man with curious neighbors. She had left the address in September, 1954, not later. And she had been pregnant.

But what happened to the lady? Left to go back to France? Or, sensing the Indiana winters, did she go to Mexico and then go wherever she was going from there?

And the baby? She was single, nineteen, monied and pregnant. Not usually a situation that lasts, intact, for the full nine months. Usually something gives, like getting married, or committing suicide, or blowing some bread to get rid of the bun in the oven.

I wondered just how pregnant she had been when she hung out the wash on Fiftieth Street.

Altogether quite fascinating.

I went to the jacket pocket that contained Leander Crystal's income records. I went through each sheet quite carefully. There weren't all that many, and while I can't claim to know what each item was, I was more adept at picking out what it wasn't. What each one wasn't was rent from the Fiftieth Street property.

Which wasn't conclusive of anything. I had no way of being certain that the records were complete or that I necessarily would have spotted rent income.

But after I went through them I was pretty sure. Sure enough to do some speculating.

Like, maybe Annie Lombard had a friend in Indianapolis after all.

But why? how? and miscellaneous other questions pertaining to the establishment of the establishment. The best question of which was the pregnancy. I knew one landlord who had not caused it.

I let it go for the moment.

* * *

I started instead on Leander Crystal's debits from before 1956.

I'm better on debits than credits. I was able to do quite a bit of positive classification. A pile of household bills, and department store bills, and tax bills. I was surprised just how unusual and outstanding the checks to Jacques Chaulet had been. They had seemed much more ordinary to me the last time I had gone through the canceled checks. I had to conclude that I was developing more skill with practice, more ability to sort out the usual from the unusual in canceled-check line. I realized how dumb I must have been not to pick out twenty thousand dollars worth of checks to one man at the beginning.

Even so, now I could class by date and by payee just what each thing went for. Like a puzzle. The things that were not blatantly ordinary centered on the house on Fiftieth Street, the trip to Europe, and the trip to New York during which Eloise was born. The house economics I had been through before: the purchase, the remodelings and the apparently rent-free status for all occupants since Crystal's purchase.

The European trip gave me a little more. They had blasted nearly nineteen thousand dollars in six and a half months. That seemed a trifle high to me for 1953-54. I wondered how easy it was to drop that kind of pocket change. I wondered if they had made any fantastic purchases. I wished I still had the letters Eloise had so graciously brought once upon a time; I wanted to go over Fleur's letters to her father. I didn't remember any suggestion of beautiful things but maybe I hadn't been looking for that sort of reference. What you notice depends so much on what you want to see.

I would have been glad to take a look at the item-by-item breakdown of that expenditure, but there wasn't any. All that was separate was a check for traveler's checks for $17,000 and a check to Matador Travel Agency for $2,941.91. That one had me too. Bit steep for plane tickets, yet not a lot for extended hotel bookings for six-plus months. Maybe tickets plus some hotels. Fair enough.

Matador had done some good business with Leander. The New York trip came through them too. September, '54. The check was dated the fifth, and paid out $307.52. That seemed high too, tacked onto a check to the Essex House Hotel for $4,102. But some folks live in style. And at the Essex House you can do just that. I figured from September 6 to November 15 made about seventy days. OK, nearly $60 a day, not bad. But a fellow begins to wonder.

161

In the process of wondering it occurred to me that Chivian had probably come along for the trip and I felt a little better. Three people can eat a lot more than two.

Hmmmm. Chivian.

At 10:12 I hit the phone. For Lafayette, Indiana. I felt like talking to my daughter's doctor.

He answered it himself. His voice was fresh, not sleepy, and he didn't sound annoyed. I wondered what he was doing and what he had been expecting. Then I realized that the man was a doctor and what I was hearing was the professional voice.

"Good evening, sir," I said in my best nasal high-pitched voice. "I'm sorry to bother you at this hour, but I am Harrison Fall, of Fall's Wigs and Falls, Inc. We are a long-established wig concern and I wondered if you would be willing to have one of our salesmen call at your home or office to show you what I believe is a quite unique line of men's wigs."

"No," he said. "I have everything I need along that line." And he hung up.

I had quite a nice line in mind. It's called the wet-mop style. It may come off in times of violent head motion, but if it does it is guaranteed to leave a clean head.

It had been my best bit of deduction in months.

I had a vision; more than a vision, a vision with sound. The bastard laughing at me, that long howl, with his hand upon his head.

But all things need checking.

It wasn't late but I had a lot of weighty stuff on my mind. Like hair. Annie's American fiancé, a bald doctor, perchance.

I perused the canceled checks for a while longer but came up with nothing. I settled for it, and at midnight I called it a day.

37

I got an early start in the morning. I headed off to Matador, where there was a very attractive girl behind the counter. I asked her if she could give me information on how much plane tickets cost round trip from Indianapolis to Paris in 1953.

She got out her book and began to thumb. Then she stopped, looked up at me, using a dainty fingertip to push up her eyelids which were drooping under the weight of bristle-brush false eyelashes, and asked, "When did you want to go again?"

"October, 1953," I said.

She squinted, and said, "Didn't that one leave already?"

I asked for the manager, who I found in a plush office on the mezzanine, and who I also found to be a bit more helpful than his help.

I identified myself and described the case I was on—running down background information on people suspected of padding expense accounts. I didn't say I was working for an important local lawyer. My demeanor bespoke the fact. I asked whether he had records on individual orders from 1953.

He said no.

So I asked instead for the price of plane travel from Indianapolis to Paris in 1953. Where had I heard that question before?

"I'm not sure," he said, "but I can give you an approximation."

I said that an approximation would be fine. He was a stolid-looking gentleman, nice clean suit, conservative cut. Moderately bald. About fifty. The world was full of them.

"Round trip I would guess about seven hundred seven and a quarter, unless you went first class."

"How about first class?"

"Another hundred."

"So if I have a check for $2,941.91 which is supposed to be the plane fares for two people to France and back then you might suggest that there would be a little something wrong with the check."

"Well, unless they went the long way round, it's more like the fare for four people. Or maybe three and a half." He smiled. He was making a joke.

I didn't smile. It didn't strike me funny. I was getting more and more idea of what had happened then and less and less idea of what was going on now.

I blundered on. "I've got another one. Round trip to New York, in 1954. What would that run?"

"Ninety, maybe a little less. That's first class."

I didn't ask what a check for $307.52 made. I did ask how possible it would be to spend $17,000 in France in six and a half months in the mid-fifties.

"That's a breeze," he said. "Even I could do that, if I had it."

"But how about without making any large purchases? I mean no houses, no diamonds."

"A little harder. But what about some big parties, some vintage champagne or some high-priced broads. No, it still would be easy."

He left out the possibility of giving the money away. Fair enough. He had been a help and I told him so.

I winked at Fan-eyes as I went out. She just stared at me. It occurred to me that she was pretty sure not to lose a contact lens. If one popped out, it would just get caught in the webbing.

I had walked to Matador; it wasn't a bad day and one could rationalize that even if the air is not good to breathe at least the exercise of walking helps balance what you lose by inhaling. Not that I was really worried about my health. It was my mental health that bothered me at the time; not having things together, a kind of insanity. A professional stage, and occupational hazard, when you are lucky enough to get some work that requires some degree of thought.

Instead of walking home I took a left and walked through downtown. Across the Monument circle, hub of Indianapolis.

Indianapolis was designed by the assistant to the man who did Washington, D.C. It's built on the same hub and spoke principle. A center traffic circle with eight spoke roads. Of course only four actually join the circle, and one of those is only two blocks long, but the principle is there, and the diagonal streets play the same kind of havoc at intersections that they do in Washington. I'll take the rectangular blocks with streets running one way and avenues running the other any old time.

I walked up to the library. Past Lyman Brothers, the site of my first job away from home. Where I took an inventory at a dollar an hour. Counting pen points, pieces of paper, multiplying by the unit value and totaling. I swore I would never work again. You can see what that got me. Owned by a nice guy though.

I didn't walk fast.

I had pieces, all kinds of pieces. Like half people. Like people who lived places and then didn't live anywhere. Like artificial insemination

164

and neurotic pregnancies. Life had to be simpler than all that. Occam's razor. Q.E.D.

It was pushing eleven. I decided to wake Miller up.

Only I didn't. He was up. Having breakfast. "What's the matter with you? Can't a fellow get away from you anywhere?"

"Only in Kentucky," I said, meaninglessly. "I was on my way home and two cars collided in an intersection I was just about to cross." They had. "So I decided not to go home, but to visit you instead. OK?"

"Jesus Christ. Make another pot of coffee, honey, we got a crazy man coming. Yeah, it's OK."

While I was in the phone box I called Andrew Elmitt's number. It rang twelve times before he answered it.

He said, "Yes?"

I identified myself and asked, "Is the parcel I left with you constituted the way you believed when we spoke?" I can talk fancy too, you know.

"Yes, it is. I'll have the exact calculations this evening after eight."

OK. Swiss accounts and half people.

I thanked the kind gentleman, hung up and waited at the bus stop trying to figure out ways I could screw him out of his hundred and fifty bucks.

Maybe break and enter.

The bus came. Miller lives in a little house on Illinois Avenue above what would be Thirty-first Street, if there were a Thirty-first Street there. It's not far from a storefront café where I first heard live jazz. You take the Meridian bus to Thirtieth Street and walk. It's the Children's Museum stop.

I walked fast because I wanted that coffee and I had to go to the john.

The real high-level talk started at the breakfast table.

"You want anything to eat?"

"No, thanks. Just the coffee."

"You haven't been here in a long time."

"I haven't been invited."

"You weren't invited this time. What's up?"

"I had to pee."

"Pee? Pee, no less. That's what a couple of years in the East does to people. They start peeing. Excuse *me* a minute. I got to go piss."

"So go piss, Sergeant." He stayed put.

"I don' got to go no mo'."

I went. When I got back we drank coffee. I don't really like coffee. But I like Miller. Janie had left the room when I came in, to clean house or something. She doesn't like me. That's why I haven't been around. I'm not a good influence, or something. No ambition, or something.

"How strong are you on getting information from foreign countries?" I asked.

He shook his head like a little mother. "You got everything there is to know from here?"

I smiled and shrugged. "How easy is it?"

"Not easy. Not without reason. That I can't just put in for. It costs a lot of money, comparatively. The chief doesn't like it."

"Less graft to spread around if you spend money on business?"

"Don't push it, Al. I can't do it without opening a file and clearing the case strategy with Captain Gartland. What stuff you want?"

"I want to locate a missing alien."

"Ah. Your immigration file. I looked through that. It's been a long time."

"If I could, I'd like to have her hometown checked to see if there has been any record of her since she got lost in this country. If she had the kind of money the consulate says, she must have had some possessions or family or something that had to be disposed of or that she had to make arrangements for after she decided to get lost. Somebody there has to know something. If she went back, fine. If she hid out here she must have given them some indication of that too."

"I can't, Al. I can't walk in one evening and open a fifteen-year-old missing-alien case just for the hell of it. I may be invisible down there, but files and foreign information requests aren't."

"OK," I said. I hadn't really expected him to do it. Not quite. Oh, all right, I had expected him to do it.

"How about checking out bodies here?"

"Any special bodies?" Janie was out of the room, he could bait me at no risk to himself. Janie is also a trifle suspicious when I am around.

166

That's because I was a good friend of the lady Miller had really wanted to marry all that time ago. It wouldn't have worked out. All parties except Janie know that.

"Yeah. Dead ones. I want my alien's prints checked against all unidentified women's bodies discovered between September first, 1954, and, say, January first, 1955.

Policemen get warped. They have strange senses of humor. I didn't even feed him a joke line and Miller laughed and laughed. "C'mon," I said, "that's in the country. You can do that."

"Any special places you want these moldy bodies checked, or all over the country?"

"All over the country. How the hell do I know where she is? You can do that, can't you? Don't they have some sort of central clearinghouse for storing prints on unidentified bodies all over the country?"

"Not that I know of yet. Not a bad idea though. I'll check it out. Until then, why don't you pick three or four cities and I'll give it a whirl."

"OK. Try Indianapolis, New York, Lafayette and Ames, Iowa. When do I get the info?"

"Big Al, believe me, if anything matches, you'll be told."

"Ah, such assurances. I haven't been so reassured since the time the dean told me that he was sure that if I worked hard I could pass all my subjects and stay in school."

"Which time was that?"

"The second time." I went to college twice. For brief periods. A year and a half and half a year, respectively.

"Little did he know."

That did it. I shut up like a clam. I was real sensitive about knowing little that noontime. And I was impatient to know more. I asked, "You going to drive me to the library now?"

"Sure."

Only he didn't, because Janie had taken the car. I believe they get along pretty well. I just bring out the worst in them. For all his passivity, which I admire, Miller would not have stuck twelve years with any woman he didn't have something going with.

I walked over to the bus stop. I was impatient. Though for what I knew not. But I could tell I was impatient because I didn't stop in the

167

Children's Museum to look at the dinosaurs and the Indian tidbits. I had half planned to when I walked by the first time. There have been times that I have done some heavy thinking in that museum. It is one of my places in Indianapolis. But not that day.

I hopped the bus and bombed back down Meridian to St. Clair Street and the library.

38

I sat in front of the Indianapolis *Star* in the browsing area. Once I tried to get them to subscribe to the *Morning Telegraph*. For the theater reviews, I said, and movie reviews. I don't know how far it got, but either the seventy-five cents a day or the fact that it really dwells on the ponies killed it. I thumbed through the *Star*.

I mulled through my own case while I skimmed the world's cases. I perused my notes.

Then I migrated to Arts where I acquired the New York *Times* microfilms for September 1 through December 31, 1954. I began to skim them. A lively era. Lots of Presidential golf.

The *Times* is inordinately long for a newspaper. So soon after I began, I stopped. Not only was I increasingly sure that miscellaneous bodies didn't make news in New York, but I was also convinced that this was not my kind of work. Damn it, Miller was going to do it for me, more efficiently and probably more rapidly.

By starting to do the crap myself, I was just being impatient. Very childish. Who was being the kid now? Good old Albert. How could I knock a poor sixteen-year-old kid for having a childish streak, when I had one myself. When everyone has them. I felt a moment of tenderness for her.

Then I reminded myself that it's the quantity of the childishness, not its existence, that counts.

I realized I was dissembling.

I put the microfilm away, back in its little boxes, and turned the viewer off. I tried to think about just what the hell I was doing and what I should be doing.

I tried to ask myself some pertinent questions. Like, Big Al, what are you meant to be doing?

It occurred to me that I was initially hired to find the biological father of Eloise Crystal.

Had I done that?

No, in all likelihood I had not. I'd found lots of other things instead. Half people and like that.

Hmmmm. Now that I thought about it, no half people at all. Those were just halves of round-trip tickets. That just meant one-way tickets.

One-way tickets. I pictured a rather slight, rather pretty little French girl walking around her apartment in New York, now, this afternoon, fifteen years later. Probably married, no doubt long over the details of how she got there in the first place. Well dowered, totally oblivious to the curiosity of the hack detective in Indianapolis who was trying to work out just where she was, just how she got nine thousand dollars to show to the consulate, and how she related to the real question that he had been hired to answer in the first place.

I picked up my notebook in one hand, and the pile of *Times* microfilms in the other, set off for the Science and Technology Division on the west end of the second floor. I almost forgot to drop the microfilm off. Such was the state of my abent-mindedness.

In Science I got down to basics. I picked out a book with the index entry "Blood types—inheritance in humans," page 297.

On page 297 I was treated to the following:

"Children's blood types are limited by the blood types of their parents."

PARENTS' blood types	CHILDREN'S blood types
O and O parents can have	O or A children
O and A	O or A
O and B	O or B
O and AB	A or B
A and A	O or A
A and B	O, A, B, or AB
A and AB	A, B, or AB
B and B	O or B
B and AB	A, B, or AB
AB and AB	A, B, or AB

OK. The Fleur and Leander I was interested in had B and O blood. That meant they could have B or O children.

And Eloise had A blood. So she was not their child.

I knew that already.

But something else bothered me. The table didn't distinguish between the parents.

I read on.

"Blood typing has been used as evidence in legal cases of questioned parenthood since 1935. Blood types are 'exclusive' tests; that is, they can not prove which two people did conceive a child, but they can prove that two people did not conceive a child. Used in conjunction with other evidence, they are often useful in establishing the correct biological parentage, especially since the identity of the mother is not normally in question. By themselves blood tests cannot distinguish the genetic contribution of the mother from that of the father, nor can it identify *all* the people who were in fact not parents of a given child."

It was enough. No, it was too much. All the facts in the world won't do a thing for you if you don't interpret them correctly, if you don't separate *fact* from presumption.

I got madder as I was putting the book back on its shelf. That's because I remembered a little part of a twelve-day-old conversation I'd had with Dr. Harry: "The adults cannot be the parents of the child."

You got to keep awake in this world.

I walked the seven blocks home. I picked up my car. It was still pretty early and there was driving to do.

I made good time out to Broadland Country Club. I'd been over the road before and I was impatient.

After I drove in the gate, I parked in the space closest to the door to the clubhouse. I recognized the lot attendant, the same one who'd been on duty my last visit. I neglected to exchange nods with him.

Inside the door was a desk with a buffalo on duty. I told him to page Leander Crystal. I gave him my name. He asked if I'd been invited by Mr. Crystal. I said I had.

At least he hadn't told me, "Mr. Crystal is on the golf course." I wondered if Crystal was still keeping up his extracurricular office on the south side. In his place I didn't know whether I would give it up or not. Maybe he was actually spending more time playing golf. I wondered if his scores were getting worse.

Crystal's face, as he came from the inner recesses to meet me, showed that the pressure was on.

"It *is* you," he said. His face was less simple than his sentence.

"Who did you expect from the name? You got some perverted friends who like to play practical jokes on you?"

"Yes," he said simply. "What do you want?"

"That's not very friendly to a fellow who has come all this way from town to give you another chance to buy him off." He looked dubious. "At a bargain price," I said. "C'mon."

"Where is there to go?" I was beginning to think the man didn't like bargains.

"Not far. To my car. Then we'll drive outside the front gate and park on the road. Then I'll ask you some questions and if the answers are right I'll bring you back here and vanish from your life."

"And if they're not right?"

"Then you'll probably kill me and I'll vanish from your life."

"Kill. You?" He shook his head and sighed. For an Army guy he seemed to present a pretty consistent notion that he wouldn't do anybody any harm. He'd said something like that before, in my office. I had it in my notebook. It's one of the things that induced me to trust him. No, not trust. It gave me the predisposition to justify what he had done, up to a point. Maybe Le Chatelier's principle applies: forced to kill in war—would never kill in peace.

I hoped.

"Surely," he said, "surely it is I who have more to fear from you than the other way. Even physically. Why do we have to go in your car?"

"Because there's not likely to be a place we can talk here in private, and even if there is I prefer to be on my own turf."

"No tape recordings?"

"I must come across a lot fancier than I feel."

We went to the car.

Outside the club gates I parked where I'd parked the last time, by the golf course.

We faced each other, each back against a door. The way you do in a

171

car when you've been poking the other party where the other party doesn't want to be poked.

"You lied to me," I said. "I don't like that."

He shrugged. He was not as I had seen him before—neither efficient protector nor tired family manager. Somewhere between, maybe a little nasty.

"What do you want?"

"All of it."

"What?"

"The whole sordid story. You can do it yourself with question and answer period later or we can do an interview. Either way, if I get it all I'm probably off your back; if I don't—" I paused, trying to think whether it would be gentlemanly to threaten him with putting IRS on his tail. He read the pause as a threat, but an undefined menace. If I had thought of it I would have done it intentionally. I liked it.

"You ask questions; I'll see if I like them."

I sighed. I was still not sure we were making progress.

"I'll start cozy," I said. "With a few yes-or-noes. You *are* Eloise's father?"

"I told you."

I sighed. I had wasted so much time and effort—all for the lack of the right question. Not "who is Eloise's father?" but "who is Eloise's mother?" I didn't feel in the mood to waste a lot of time now. "This one will show you the ball park we are in. Eloise's mother was Annie Lombard, was she not?"

I had regained his attention. Recrystallized my position. He squirmed as if the handle of the car door was rabbit punching him. Then he said, "Yes."

"All right. You see progress has been made. Who was the father, the biological father?"

But the progress was limited. He didn't answer the question. He waited a few seconds, then said, "Just why the hell should I talk to you? Just what the hell do I have to gain from telling you anything?"

"That depends," I said.

"On what?"

"On what the whole story is. I don't want anything from you, Crystal, except the truth and some reason to believe you will love and care for Eloise for the next few years. If you are straight, and if I find

172

out what I want to know, then I will return you to your country club, to your golf, to your secret office and to your whores, and I will leave your life forever."

"As simple as that."

"As simple as that. I am assuming that such a deal will appeal to you *if* you are not a wicked man with violence in his past. I believe you are not actively wicked, or I wouldn't be here."

"Wicked," he mimicked me, and tried to laugh. "OK, what do you want to know?"

"Who is Eloise's father?"

"I am."

"Wasn't that a bit sticky?" He paused. I continued. "In Toulon, with your wife there?"

He shook his head in what I took egotistically to be wonderment.

"We needed a child," he said.

"To conform to the terms of Estes' will."

"But Fleur is sterile. She can't have children. I can't tell you what learning that did to us."

"Chivian conducted the examination and tests?"

"Yes. I knew him from the Army. We were both—" he stopped again. But I could imagine. They were both young, ambitious. It would be impossible to reconstruct how much planning had gone into their cultivation of Joshua Graham, how much agreement there had been to share any progress either made up the money ladder.

"So you imported Chivian?"

"Yes. After four years with Fleur I knew we had trouble. I knew I wasn't sterile. It was driving Fleur crazy." He was talking more easily. "We couldn't let Estes know about it, and there weren't too many places in the world he would let us go that we could also do what we had to. In the Army Chivian and I could get most things done. So we went back to see some people we knew there, in France. When we got to Toulon we looked up Jacques Chaulet, and after a while Jacques found Annie."

In a sense I was blackmailing the man. The story was an emotional one. It was costing him.

"It seemed so clear then," he said. "Anyway Jacques found Annie. She was just what we were looking for. Unattached and without prospects. Jacques had known her family. Her father was dead. She was

173

burned by the bomb that killed her mother. You can imagine some of the things she'd already been through late in the war and after it. She'd already had illegitimate twins, so we knew she was fertile."

"She was perfect," I said.

He nodded. "So for convenience, I impregnated her. We figured that if I was the father the child would be more likely to look like us. Annie doesn't look much like Fleur."

"Not many women do," I said uselessly. It was an emotional story for me too. Lots of wild, conflicting feelings, but a few of them favored Leander Crystal. "What then?"

"Once we were sure Annie was pregnant we all came back. I set Annie up in a house I have—"

"On Fiftieth Street. Mrs. Forebush's house. I know." I was showing off, but information that had come so hard . . .

It registered, and reinforced his resignation.

I asked, "Who was the bodyguard?"

"Bodyguard? Oh, I see. Chivian lived with her."

"Lived with?"

"Separate rooms. We never took advantage of her."

I thought of the pictures in his pornography collection, but I let it pass. In no way could it have been easy for them all for those months. Not for Annie or for the Crystal conspirators. The time had to be passed.

"What did you pay her?"

"Ten thousand dollars."

"And Jacques?" I knew, but I was already cross-checking the story.

"Twenty." Check.

"Weren't you afraid of Jacques?"

"I was. But Chivian has some information on him which he said would keep him in line. I don't know what it was but I haven't heard from him, except once offering a business deal."

"And did you take it?"

"No. It was illegal." With dignity.

"What about Chivian?"

"We have a long-term arrangement. I helped set him up and I give him an annuity. It hasn't been excessive. He knows that the money is Fleur's and that he lives at least as well as I do.

It was time, yet I hesitated. My hole card.

174

"And the Swiss account? Does Chivian have one of those too?"

He shook his head. He rubbed his eyes, his wrinkly forehead, and then his temples.

"You know," I said, "or do you, that I have another set of prints of the pictures I took in your office."

"I didn't know. But I can see now that you must have."

I sidetracked. "Did you steal your file from my office or did you have it done?"

He smiled weakly. "I did it myself."

"You missed my second set of pictures sitting on my desk." I didn't tell him about the set Miller had kept. I didn't think that he would like my telling him that anybody else knew about any of this. "Why did you steal the file when you did?"

"Chivian insisted. When you made that appointment to see him he was sure you had decided not to take the money."

"Were you sure?"

"No. I didn't like it, but there is something about you." The biggest ego boost of my day. "I thought we should wait awhile longer."

I said quietly, "When did you plan to leave?" We both knew I was talking about his Swiss cache again.

"Not for a while. Not really till Eloise was older."

"Would you ever have told her?"

"All this?" He laughed harshly. "No. Never. I love that child, as much as I can love. This is not the kind of thing one tells one's daughter. Under ordinary circumstances." Right, but neither is she an ordinary child.

"Was Fleur really pregnant?"

"You may not believe this, but I don't know."

"I don't believe that."

"You have to understand that things have changed over the years. Some sort of bond has grown between my wife and Henry Chivian which I would never have imagined possible years ago. We get older, I guess. I do know that he had been treating her with fertility drugs."

"Without telling you?"

He gave a little laugh. "Yes. That's an example of his idea of a joke. I'm never there when he comes to see Fleur. And he comes every week or two."

"And the miscarriage?"

175

"If she was pregnant, then she had one. I am sure that whatever the truth, Fleur thought she was pregnant. She takes everything that he gives her."

"But Chivian doesn't know about the money you have tucked away?"

"No. I would be getting away from him as much as anybody."

"Leaving Fleur to him?"

"She'd still have lots of money, which he likes. He's still a doctor, which she likes. I don't know."

"What happened to Annie?"

"She went back to France to live on her money. Jacques was supposed to look out for her."

"Tell me what happened in New York."

"After Estes' funeral we all went to New York because Fleur couldn't stand to stay. We would have gone soon anyway. Fleur was going crazy having to dress up in a pregnancy costume whenever she came out of her room. The worst was when the old man wanted to feel her belly for the baby. Really quite hideous."

"You went to New York."

"So we went to New York. We checked in, with me and Annie as Mr. and Mrs. Crystal, and Fleur and Henry as Dr. and Mrs. Chivian. When Annie's time came, she went to the hospital as Mrs. Crystal; Henry delivered the baby. After a couple of weeks Fleur and Henry and I, and Eloise, came back to Indianapolis. And Annie went back to France."

"The Immigration Department has no record of Annie leaving the country."

"I don't know anything about that, but she did leave. We bought her a ticket."

As if that guaranteed it.

"OK," I said, and prepared to drive.

"OK what?"

"OK, why don't you go and play some golf and I'll finish up a few odds and ends and let you know."

He shrugged and became a passenger. "I still don't understand," he said.

Nor was he alone. "Think of it this way. You feel better now that you've got it all off your chest, right?"

"No," he said.

I dropped him in the parking lot at Broadland.

176

I drove home slowly. I felt almost too certain the man had been telling the truth. It's not safe to have confidence in people. I might have been more skeptical had he answered my questions in the commanding manner he had used in all our previous exchanges. But apparently resigned and in my own model '58?

I wanted very much to believe him, because getting truth from him would mean that I had paid him back for underestimating me.

But I wasn't happy. If I was playing revenge, it was really Chivian that I wanted. But more than that I was becoming aware, for the first time, that the case was nearly over. I would take the information Crystal had given me; I would check some of it, somehow. It would check. I would go my way. It made me feel tired. It made me feel poor.

I indulged myself with a little daydream. Convinced that Albert is an honorable man, Leander Crystal decides to make Albert the free, spontaneous, unstringed gift of fifty thousand dollars.

And Albert takes it.

A nice daydream, based on two equally unlikely events.

I would run straight to the bank and draw it in cash. I would buy my little girl the biggest, baddest teddy bear in the whole world.

39

It never occurred to me that I had visitors until I stepped into the outer office. I hadn't seen their car; I hadn't heard them jawing. Nothing.

Cops. Bags of cops, like three. Only they seemed like more since I didn't know any of them, neither the two uniformed gentlemen, nor the plain-clothes gentleman.

I said aloud, "As my father told my mother after I was born, it's not at all what I expected."

I was all ready to continue with a recital of my prices. I didn't get the chance. The aliens were not entirely friendly.

"Where the hell have you been? We've been looking for you for an hour and a half," said the plain-clothes gentleman.

"I would have baked a cake," I said. I'm good at returning fast-growing free-blooming hostility. I hadn't asked them in.

177

The plain-clothes gentleman continued to do the talking. That I approved of. I've long believed that patrolmen should be seen and not heard. And I much prefer talking to people whose guns are obscured by a layer of cheap suit. For me, out of sight helps out of mind.

He said, "All right, give us the story."

With anybody else I would have started on Goldilocks and the Three Bears. But they wouldn't have liked it.

I had had an active day, lots of driving and talking and strategizing. I didn't feel like wasting my breath.

I went around to the business side of my desk and sat down. The patrolman sitting on the desk edge didn't get the message, so I maneuvered my right foot so that it rested firmly but gently on his posterior.

"OK. You two bears go sit on the floor and enjoy some porridge. You, plain-clothes bear, identify yourself and then tell me just what the fuck is going on here."

I must inspire confidence. They did what I told them. The plain-clothes cop showed me the ID for a Captain Wilson Gartland. The uniforms went by the door and sat on a bench I have there. I knew the name, Gartland. I was talking to Miller's very own captain.

He was not exactly sweetness and light. After he repocketed his ID, he took my feet and threw them off my desk.

"Listen to me, Samson, and listen good. We got a murder here and we want to know where you fit."

"A murder?" I don't know what I was expecting, but it wasn't that.

"You want I should spell it?"

All I said was no. Real people don't get involved in murders, especially not nonviolent ones. It knocked my rosy little daydream notion of things askew.

Gartland was not considerate of my surprise. He shook his head and pursed his lips. "Believe me, Samson, you better not get cute with me."

If I'd worked out any reason for their presence in my life I'd just thought Gartland didn't like my getting information from Miller and had come to give me some trouble for it.

"Please," I said, "start at the beginning. Who?"

I guess cops don't get asked "please" very often. Gartland said, "You get one of my men to put in a check of fingerprints with dead bodies

178

and he comes up with a match. A dead body sitting around unidentified for sixteen years and you walk in one day and turn the key. Do you expect me to believe that you don't know what's going on? So spill, shamus. You can do it here or downtown."

In adversity he was getting trite. We were already downtown, for openers—just not at his house. And "shamus" went out with the bustle. But I forgave him. "Where's Miller?" I said.

"I'm handling this now."

That didn't seem reasonable. "I don't talk to anybody but Miller."

"For crying out loud." I guess I hurt his feelings, but I could tell what he was thinking. He was balancing the importance of giving Miller a sixteen-year-old murder case against the convenience of not having to break me.

I offered a sop. "I'll tell Miller everything I know." I was glad I'd played tough when I came in. I knew he could break me with a feather, but he didn't. I break easy because I'm afraid of guns. Not that they go around shooting witnesses in murder cases in Indianapolis. Not usually anyway. Not white witnesses. Not before they get the information out of them.

"You take me to Miller," I said, "and I'll spill everything I know." Shamus indeed.

Gartland sighed. He waved to his uniformed associates. "Take him in," he said, in a tone which sounded like he was carrying out a threat when he really was giving in to me. Subtle guys, these captains.

The ride from my office to cop center was less than two blocks, but they didn't speak to me at all. I appreciated the silence. It gave me a little chance to reorient myself. Especially with respect to Leander Crystal. Either he had conned me a second time or even he hadn't known everything that went on. I got a rudimentary notion of how I wanted to play it, and I was glad that Miller owed me for getting him back on the case.

At headquarters Miller was not hard to locate. There is nobody more present than a man who has been taken off a big case but who thinks there might be the slightest hope of getting back on it. I was his hope. Very touching, and I could always get additional leverage by reporting him for stealing cars as a kid.

Gartland was not gracious about turning me over to him. And he was even less gracious when he found out I wanted to talk to Miller alone. But finally we shooed the surplus uniforms away and had a friendly chat.

"Where was it?" I asked him.

"Your alien's prints matched a body in New York."

I nodded as if I already knew. He picked up some paper.

"A previously unidentified female body discovered in Central Park, New York. November 23, 1954. Caucasian. Aged twenty to thirty. 5 feet 3. Brown hair. Hazel eyes. Dead a few days. Skull fracture and mutilations. She was probably knocked out, strangled and then cut to ribbons in the area between her waist and her knees."

It chilled and shocked me. I rocked back and forth in my seat.

"New York covered the match with a note. They say they never checked the corpse's prints with the FBI—that's where they file aliens' prints—because they didn't have any reason to believe she was foreign. In the park, in the condition she was in, they figured her for a whore cut up by some kind of maniac. When nobody came looking for her they closed it unsolved."

I nodded grimly. People get killed every minute somewhere in the world. It doesn't bother you because you don't know about it. This killing sixteen years ago bothered me terribly. I did know things about it, things other people didn't know. Like why she was killed, who she had been, and why she had been killed in that particular way at that particular time.

"Al, New York wants to know how we matched it with Annie Lombard. So does the Justice Department."

"So does everybody, if I judge the look in your eyes correctly."

"I can't help it, Al. You know what this could mean to me. You know probably better than anyone."

I wished I could shut him up at that moment. I knew what it meant to him all right. But I wished that I could have been there in 1954 to stop it, because it can't have been nice. I wished I could keep the billions of people who get pushed around every day from having to take it anymore. I wished I wasn't unimportant to everybody except me, and I wished I wasn't going to die someday.

I said, "Yeah, I know. I've just been figuring out how to go about it. There are people I don't want to have hurt."

"That girl, Annie Lombard, she got hurt in the worst way, Al."

The platitude made me mad. Who the hell knew that better than I did? Who knew better about the pictures of the girl in the progressing stages of pregnancy, and who knew better about her daughter?

"Don't play the cop ploys with me, Jerry. Don't do it. You are going to get credit for this, but it goes my way or not at all. It's hung around for sixteen years, and, by God, if you don't watch out it's going to hang around for another sixteen."

When I said it I meant it, but it didn't take long for me to remember all the records and files I had around, not to mention my notebook. Laid out like that even Gartland could figure out enough of it.

Miller felt my passion, but he was evaluating his own situation. "It's hard. You know that."

"Bull. I had to con you into getting the things for me in the first place and now you're acting like it was all your idea. Just because I stumbled on it doesn't mean that you're any dumber than anybody else or any less fit to be a lieutenant."

We had communicated at last. It's one of the facts of life that friends are not perfect. But you learn to patch up the breaches. A little booze. A few reminiscences.

There was a knock on the door. Gartland stuck his face in. It seemed only seconds since we'd seen it last. If Miller had been in doubt about our understanding, Gartland's frowning mug resolved it.

"Get out," Miller addressed his captain. "We'll let you know."

The face withdrew and we got down to business. I gave it all to him, in essence as Leander had told it to me. In chronological order, not the way I'd found it.

Then I told him that I wanted us to go and visit Leander Crystal.

"But he lied to you till it was coming out of your ears," he said.

I shrugged. It's not that I had any big master plan which would identify all the guilty and clear all the innocent. But I wanted to talk to Crystal again before we pulled the rug out. I had to have a chance to find out whether my gut reaction—to trust the man—had really been as far off base as it seemed it was. One of the things which distinguishes children from adults is the confidence to make and trust one's own value judgments. When I decide to trust someone it's disorienting to find out he's not trustworthy.

Miller thought we should just go pick them all up and then straighten everything out later.

181

But he acceded to my wishes. That was the deal.

We went out and told Gartland. If Miller didn't like it, Gartland hated it. But since he still didn't know the details all he could do was rant about what would happen to Miller if something went wrong.

Miller played cool. What else could he do but go along with me, he told Gartland. Little as they both liked it I was calling the shots. And in his opinion if they didn't act fast they might lose the killer.

It was all a subtle reminder that Gartland had opted to bring Miller back in, and that the consequences were ultimately still his.

We requested and got four patrolmen and two cars.

We left. Gartland hated it.

40

Miller and I rode together in the back of one unmarked car. The other followed us. We pulled up in tandem in front of the Crystal house. If Chivian was there, his car was not out front. It probably didn't matter. Whatever Crystal had told him about our afternoon session, they couldn't be expecting this.

As we got out I waved the second car back along Jefferson Boulevard, to get it more out of sight. They were there in case someone left the house by car. The other two cops were to post outside, front and back. Only Miller would come in with me. I wanted to give Leander Crystal as much benefit of doubt as possible. But also to protect Miller in case Crystal didn't deserve such benefits.

"If anybody does come out," I warned the two cops to be posted at front and back, "warn them, identify yourself, fire a warning shot, but do not, repeat, do not shoot them."

They looked at Miller. He nodded. "Unless they are threatening your life." He checked the load in his gun. The patrolmen did the same. Then they walked to their positions.

After giving them a little time Miller and I walked silently across the lawn to the front door.

It was about eight thirty, dark. Lights shone upstairs and downstairs to our right. Muted lights showed elsewhere.

I felt the kind of majesty that a big house can have, especially when you are walking across the lawn as if you owned it. The Crystal Palace.

Leander Crystal answered the door. He stood for a moment taking in the fact that there were two of us. Then he functioned. "Come in." He led us toward the living room. Just as well. It was the only place in the house with which I felt any familiarity, felt comfortable.

The comfort did not last. Seated in the living room was Henry Chivian, MD. He got up as we came in. He grinned. He couldn't have been there long or he wouldn't have been grinning from what Leander told him I knew. Or would he?

"Where is everybody?" I asked as we sat down. Us two facing them two. Leander said, "Fleur and Eloise are upstairs. What can I do for you? And who is this gentleman?"

"This is Jerry Miller. He is a friend of mine and he is also a sergeant of police."

"Police!" He stood up. I forgave him that. Anyone would be nervous on a day his deceptions of sixteen years had been coming down around his ears. What I had to establish was just how nervous he was.

"Sit down, Mr. Crystal." I used my fatherly voice. He sat down. Thankfully, Chivian had ceased to smile. I wanted to jump over the table between us and pull off his wig.

Leander did the talking for their side.

"I don't understand, Samson. This afternoon—" He stopped himself. "What does he know?"

I talked for our side. I spoke quietly, concentrating on his face. "He knows everything that you told me this afternoon."

He just sat and shook his head. "I don't understand. I thought we had an arrangement." Chivian clearly didn't know anything. He was relaxed, grinning again.

"Things aren't quite what they were this afternoon." Still quietly. "I've found out about Annie."

He looked at me. "What about Annie?" Chivian's grin fell like a bomb. He lurched forward to the edge of the couch.

"I've found her body."

"Her *body*!" said Crystal. "Where? When? When was she. . . ?"

I'm not infallible, but it was good enough for me.

"In New York," I said. "Central Park."

"But when? I don't understand what this has to do with. . . ?" And

183

then I believe a wave of understanding broke inside his head. It showed in his eyes. I helped it.

I said, "Sixteen years ago. They found her November twenty-third."

"Oh, my God," he said. His head was down. In his hands.

It must have been then that I began to hear a high-pitched laugh begin. It was low in volume to begin with. I didn't quite notice it at the time. It's just on recollection that I have figured out when it began.

"Oh, my God," he repeated. "No!" I was concentrating on Crystal. I remember wondering if he was crying, or what. I sensed tension coming into his body. And it was then that I consciously realized the sound was a laugh.

It was hideous and growing and high-pitched. I call it a laugh because my vocabulary isn't all that good. But it wasn't a scream. It was getting louder. For a few instants I couldn't find the direction. I looked at Chivian but he was looking around, too. I guess I was convinced that it was coming from Crystal. But a second after I became conscious of the sound and of Crystal's tensing, it all began to happen.

His head came up and I had a moment to realize that his mouth was closed and his eyes were somehow not involved in a noise like that.

It was rising and loud and there was a bursting sort of sound. Like through a door.

Like behind me.

I have a visual memory of Leander Crystal diving toward my right. Somehow stronger than diving. Hurling himself.

Then all I remember is her being on me. Turning me or my turning in reaction to her. But somehow turning so I saw three or four flashes.

They say that she got me six times and that must have been what the flashes were.

They call knives cold and metallic but all I felt was a hot poker ripping into my right side. And ripping again. And again.

I have a faint notion of a red moment, of red passing before my eyes, but I wouldn't swear to it. It might have been my blood. They say there was a lot of it. Or her hair.

I don't know. All I know is that at that moment I decided to lie down and go to sleep.

41

How they got her off me I don't know. They don't know. Miller says that he thinks Crystal may have deflected her when he dived for her legs. Crystal doesn't agree. He feels like he just rolled right off her, that's how hard she was coming. They agree that somehow they did get her off, knock her off, or she decided to leave. She got up from my body and ran for the door from the living room to the front, out the house. There is disagreement about whether she was still making that sound, but there is no disagreement that it was just as she was going through the living-room door that Miller shot her.

He had had a lot of trouble, he says now. Trouble getting the gun out of his holster. When he did shoot she was virtually through the door. He thought he had missed her. But the coroner says he didn't. The bullet went through the door and into her back. Apparently there were wood splinters near the entry hole. It didn't kill her immediately, but it was a mortal wound, they say, being near the backbone. I just wonder what kind of world it can be when "mortal" wounds are fatal.

Nobody knows when Chivian got out, but he did, and true to his devious character he went through the back to the garage and his car. They picked him up about eight miles away—the patrol cops.

I do know, from the cop posted out front, that Fleur came out the front door as if she were sprinting. He was amazed to find out later that she had a bullet in her, especially a police .38. But the door must have taken some of the sting out of it.

The kid's name is Fred Wilsky; he's not a bad kid. He says that he heard the screaming and the shot and saw her coming out the front door all about the same time. He says he drew his gun, but that without appearing to have seen him she turned the other way and ran toward the street. He says he may have forgotten to identify himself as a policeman, but he doesn't know. He says he fired a warning shot and she didn't break stride. Then he says he didn't know what else to do but run after her.

That amazes me. If it had been me I would have had that gun up and shot her full of holes. I swear I would. So help me. But maybe I'm

185

prejudiced. I don't like punctured lungs and broken ribs and chopped liver. And blood, and being alive now only because she got the right side of my body and not my left side. I lack a certain degree of self-control. I would have made her into mincemeat.

Fred was just following the orders he had been given. That I had given him.

She was about halfway down the block and Fred was about twenty yards past the front door himself when Miller got there and screamed to him, "Get her, get her." I guess in person it was a less ambiguous instruction than it reads.

Fred got her. When I talked to him he was upset about having shot a woman, but the coroner says she was dead anyway, would have been in a few minutes.

Inside the house Crystal was calling an ambulance and Miller says it was for me. Before it got there he went up and got Eloise.

She says that she had thought it was Leander who was hurt, that she knew that her mother had done something, from her laugh, but that she thought it had been Leander for making her get artificially inseminated. Miller says that Eloise was pretty cool considering, and that she sat by me for a moment until the ambulance came.

Oh, lots of people came to the hospital to tell me cheerful tales.

But not everyone who visited me in the hospital came to tell me things. Captain Gartland, for one. He came two days after the fact and he was literally unwilling to tell me the time of day. I wasn't all that interested; I inquired only because from the way I felt it had to be three in the morning.

He said he had to have some answers and had to have them now. I told him to go away. Then I pretended to go to sleep. When he didn't leave I took the plunge and rang for the nurse. I started coughing when she came in. She did the dirty work and shooed Gartland out. But it hurt, to cough.

Everything hurt. I won't give you a day-by-day hospital report, but don't believe movies that have guys doing talking a few minutes before they die. That close you don't feel like talking. It was bad enough that my mother closed Bud's for a couple of days to come hold my hand.

About a week later I saw Gartland and did talk to him. I had to feel a little sympathy for him. He had everybody on his back. Like New York about Annie. And the city officials and press about the circumstances surrounding the death of the daughter of Estes Graham. And the IRS people about Leander's tax situation. And later on, the Army was interested in looking into Joshua's death, and someone from the city talked about digging up Estes.

Big muck, big muckrakers.

Miller says he thinks Chivian and Fleur killed Annie without Leander's knowledge. That Fleur probably did the actual cutting, having seen the way she went for me.

Chivian's lawyer has told the press that Fleur must have killed Annie alone; that if she had any help it was from Leander; that his client was in no way involved; and that if Chivian was involved he was an unwitting accomplice.

Gartland wanted me to help him show they were all in on it.

The IRS wanted to get Crystal for avoiding taxes on the money he had stockpiled in Switzerland. Andrew Elmitt saw that in the paper and called me in the hospital. It was ridiculous, he said. According to his analysis Leander recorded the money and paid taxes on it. He got it simply by stealing it from Fleur. He prepared a letter to that effect which would show how Leander's records proved it. He wanted to know whether if he sent it to me unsigned, I would forward it to IRS and keep his name out of it. I did.

My time in the hospital was unreal. I kept thinking about strange things, once I got used to the fact that I was actually there. I remembered that Kevin Loughery played basketball for the Baltimore Bullets against the New York Knicks in the 1969 NBA play-offs while he was recovering from a collapsed lung and a broken rib. I still find that hard to conceive. I spent three months in the hospital and I didn't even feel like watching basketball on TV.

42

My last day on the case was February 20, 1971. It was a big day. I had been feeding myself for three weeks—including buying the food and cooking it. I had been answering the phone and talking civilly. Joking with people sometimes. That morning I had actually walked to the library and back, all by myself. I took out a book, the whole bit. I felt pretty whole and moderately functional. Though I spent three hours resting after I got back, I felt pretty proud of myself.

By three thirty I got up again. By four I had eaten an orange and some potato chips and I was sitting at my desk in the office. Showing off. And thinking about whether maybe I ought to get married again. It might be the time. My woman was feeling sorry for me and she might give in over her better judgment. Besides a wife, I would be gaining another daughter. Her girl is twelve.

At four fifteen I had company.

A rather subdued teen-ager, a girl, opened the door and walked right in.

"I'm glad you're here," she said. Without a moment's hesitation she sat down in my very, very dusty client's chair.

"Nowhere else, honey," I said. I was much more relaxed than I had been the first time I talked to Eloise Crystal. So was she, until she started looking me over. I was redecorated, though I try to hide it. A little cast for the right arm here, a little brace for the ribs there. Very fetching, and fortunately impermanent. I've even found that it's harder to drink orange juice left-handed.

"I didn't realize you were still—"

"Trussed up? Yeah. For a while yet. They had to get me out of the hospital because my insurance only went through ninety days."

"You mean you have to pay?"

"It's not settled yet. My man says that I was on police business. The police say that I'm not a cop. We're playing it safe. I'm out of the

188

hospital and we're not talking about it all until after I've testified in the trial. But how are you? How have you been?"

"OK. Pretty good."

She was lying of course, as children will. I knew she had had a hard time, physically on top of mentally. With her environmental mother dead and her father in jail they had kept her in a guardianship home for two weeks. Then, when I got around to asking Miller about her, I suggested that they put her in Mrs. Forebush's house. When they checked it out, they found Mrs. Forebush had been down at the station asking about the child every day since the story hit the papers. She had come to the hospital too, only she came before I was seeing anybody. It was a month before I was allowed to see anybody besides immediate family and cops. And you know what that meant: 99 percent cops.

"Shouldn't you be in school?"

She gave me a smile, a decent one. "It's Saturday." We sat and looked at each other.

"Happy birthday," I said. "A little belated, but I haven't forgotten."

Before I knew it she was next to me and crying. I rose to meet her and took her in my arm. I pulled her close, and I seemed to squeeze tears out. I knew I wasn't hurting her. I was still too weak to hurt people. The pain was inside, and it was raw and it was sore and it was not healing very fast.

How can you comfort someone who has been hurt worse than you ever have? A poor little girl, who would always be beautiful to me, and young, and daughtery.

She cried and cried and cried. I didn't get tired, standing there, holding her, and listening to her heart.

And to mine. When she finally subsided we sat down again and she pulled the chair over to mine. We sort of knew where we'd been and where we were going. We each had a new family, of sorts. I would teach her to drink whiskey, in time. A couple of weeks at least. When she got married, she would invite me and my other daughters to come and take a trip on her yacht. I don't know; it's clear enough to me.

When she left to go back to Mrs. Forebush's, it was about five thirty. My nap time. But instead I went into the back room, clanked around until I found my field glasses, and trotted, as well as I was able, to the

189

office next door. I rested on the window ledge. I didn't open the window to lean out, but she had crossed the street and I could watch her walking, slowly, in the general direction of the circle and the bus out to Fiftieth Street. You have to be nostalgic sometimes; you have to round out the old times to get yourself ready for the new.

MURDER, MYSTERY, AND MAYHEM FROM MICHAEL Z. LEWIN

Edgar Allan Poe Award-nominee Michael Z. Lewin receives unanimous critical acclaim. Cheered Ross Macdonald, "Mr. Lewin writes with style and sensibility and wit...he has a fine poetic sense of detail which lights up every page." Here are six of his best private eye thrillers.

☐ **ASK THE RIGHT QUESTION** 0-446-40021-1/$4.95 ($5.95 in Canada)

☐ **THE WAY WE DIE NOW** 0-446-40023-8/$4.95 ($5.95 in Canada)

☐ **THE ENEMIES WITHIN** 0-446-40024-6/$4.95 ($5.95 in Canada)

☐ **THE SILENT SALESMAN** 0-446-40025-4/$4.99 ($5.99 in Canada)

☐ **MISSING WOMAN** 0-446-40026-2/$4.99 ($5.99 in Canada)

☐ **OUT OF SEASON** 0-446-40027-0/$4.99 ($5.99 in Canada)

The Mysterious Press name and logo are trademarks of Warner Books, Inc.

**Warner Books P.O. Box 690
New York, NY 10019**

Please send me the books I have checked. I enclose a check or money order (not cash), plus 95¢ per order and 95¢ per copy to cover postage and handling,* or bill my ☐ American Express ☐ VISA ☐ MasterCard. (Allow 4-6 weeks for delivery.)

___Please send me your free mail order catalog. (If ordering only the catalog, include a large self-addressed, stamped envelope.)

Card # _____

Signature _____ Exp. Date _____

Name _____

Address _____

City _____ State _____ Zip _____

*New York and California residents add applicable sales tax.   507